STRIKING OUT

STRIKING OUT

WILL WEAVER

HarperCollins*Publishers*

With thanks to Carlton Anderson,
coach and English teacher,
and Mike Crocker, sportswriter.

Library of Congress Cataloging-in-Publication Data
Weaver, Will.
  Striking out / Will Weaver.
    p.   cm.
  Summary: Since the death of his older brother, thirteen-year-old Billy Baggs
has had a distant relationship with his father, but life on their farm in northern
Minnesota begins to change when he starts to play baseball.
  ISBN 0-06-023346-X. — ISBN 0-06-023347-8 (lib. bdg.)
  [1. Farm life—Minnesota—Fiction.   2. Baseball—Fiction.   3. Fathers and sons—
Fiction.   4. Death—Fiction.   5. Minnesota—Fiction.]   I. Title.
PZ7.W3623Sv   1993   93-565
[Fic]—dc20   CIP
                                                                                  AC

Typography by Al Cetta
1   2   3   4   5   6   7   8   9   10
❖
First Edition

*To Caitlin Rose Weaver
and Owen Harte Weaver*

PROLOGUE
1965

Billy's brother, Robert, would have been thirteen that summer.

But here's how it happened.

The accident.

Billy and Robert were home on the farm by themselves. Their parents were gone to town, the father for plow parts and their mother for groceries. A brief town trip. There was nothing unusual about this.

At home Robert was disking with the big tractor. It was spring. Spring was the shortest season in Minnesota. It was important to keep the tractor going. To put in the hours. Dawn to dark, dark to dawn. Fields did not get finished otherwise. They did not get plowed, disked, harrowed and planted unless someone kept the tractor moving.

Robert, the older brother, was twelve. He would be thirteen in August. So he was old enough. He was big enough for tractor work. Robert had disked all that spring. There was no reason, then, why he could not keep disking while Abner and Mavis were gone to town.

Eight-year-old Billy was supposed to clean out the hayloft. Get it ready for first cutting. That was Billy's chore while they were gone. One hour, they said. They would be back in one hour.

It was hot and dusty in the hayloft. Billy worked and thought about his brother. Robert got all the good jobs. He got to drive the tractor while Billy got to sweep the loft and muck out calf pens. It wasn't fair. Not fair at all. He went to the haymow door to watch Robert on the tractor in the field. The sky was blue and the tractor rumbled and left a thick cloud of dust.

Billy sighed and turned back to the loft. The dim, gloomy loft. Along the eaves were skeletons of beavers and muskrats and minks and foxes. These were from his father's winter trapping. After skinning, he threw the carcasses up for the cats. The cats chewed on them all winter. Chewed on the red meat until spring, when there were only gut sacks and bones and beaver tails left. With a fork Billy pitched the stinking remains out the door. Once he stopped to look at the long yellow teeth of a beaver; the skull smelled and there were white maggots in the eyeholes. He pitched it, too. Below, Skinner, their dog, crunched bones with his teeth. A crackling, crunching sound. Billy went again to the door. To watch Robert in the field.

Billy kept working, sweeping out the dusty hay chaff. He went again and again to the door for fresh air. In the field, under the blue sky, Robert kept disking. Kept the tractor rumbling. Kept the gray dirt rolling up in broad, black stripes. At field's end, when Robert made the turn, the round iron plates of the disk flashed in the sunlight.

Billy threw down his broom. Who was going to check the hayloft? Not his father. Not Robert. Nobody, at least for a while. He climbed down from the itchy hayloft and rode his bike to the field.

He arrived just as Robert came past. The big John Deere, their heaviest tractor, had an open cab, and Robert stood upright on the platform. No enclosed cabs on the Baggs farm. Cab tractors, with their radios and their air conditioning—those were for the big operators. The rich farmers. Not for the Baggs family. Besides, in a cab how could you see the ground? How could you see the rocks that rose up? How could you hear a bearing when it gave out or an axle when it snapped? No fancy cab for them, and no roll bar either; their John Deere was built in the days before those things were made. It was an old, rumbling green barge of a tractor plenty good enough for plowing and disking. And Robert stood upright at the wheel like a captain on his ship.

Billy waved.

Robert waved. And passed by.

Each round Robert came by Billy waved to him.

Each round Robert waved back.

Each time the tractor passed, Billy disgustedly pitched a rock at the grating, grinding disk. "Anybody can disk," he said to Skinner. "Why does he get to disk and I don't?"

The next time Robert came by, Billy waved and

waved until Robert stopped. Billy shouted up to him. He asked Robert if he could ride along.

"No," Robert said.

"Please. Just one round."

Robert glanced back at the yard. His hair was bright yellow and curly beneath his cap. "All right," he said, "but only one round."

So Billy got his ride.

He was mostly happy.

Halfway downfield Billy shouted again above the tractor noise.

"What?" Robert said.

"Can I steer?"

Robert frowned, but made way to let Billy hold the wheel for a while. Billy sat between Robert's legs and steered. He was happier still.

At field's end Billy shouted again.

"What now?" Robert said.

"Can I shift? Can I try shifting and steering at the same time?"

"You're too little," Robert said.

"No I'm not."

"Yes you are."

"No I'm not."

"Yes you are."

"Please?"

Robert checked his watch, then looked at Billy. "If I let you try it then you'll vamoose?"

"Forever," Billy said. "I'll leave you alone forever."

Robert stood up to make more room for Billy. He gave Billy instructions. "Push in the clutch," he said.

Billy pushed in the clutch pedal. It was heavy. It had a strong spring. He could hardly push it down.

"Now bring up the rpms," Robert said.

Billy opened the throttle partway.

"Now let it out real slow."

Billy tried—but that is when it happened.

Something happened.

Billy's leg muscle cramped. Maybe that was it. His leg cramped and seized and gave way.

Or maybe his tennis shoe slipped. Slipped over the top of the clutch.

And the great iron tractor roared and lurched forward. It did so because a tractor does only what it is told. A tractor does not care who is at the wheel. It cares only about its orders.

Orders from the clutch.

Orders from the main gearbox.

Orders from the splines and pinions in the transfer case.

Orders from the axles that reach out and turn the wheels.

If it is told to go, the tractor goes. It does not care who is hanging on. It does not care who is falling.

Billy remembered Robert's head jerking backward. His yellow hair moving past Billy. He remembered Robert's hand grabbing at his shoulder, at his neck, scraping past but not getting a grip. Not getting a grip on anything. He remembered Robert off balance and falling.

He did not grab for his brother because his hands were frozen to the wheel. His brother fell and he did not even grab for him. He was scared, or it happened too fast, or both.

Robert went down between the tractor and the disk. Turning, Billy saw Robert's head glance off the steel drawbar. Saw his eyes roll white and his body crumple onto the dirt.

The gray dirt.

The dirt that had not been cut and turned by the disk.

Billy screamed.

Screamed Robert's name.

And one of Robert's hands came up. Came up and grabbed the drawbar. Hung on. He hung on for a few feet. And then the hand was gone. Robert was gone. Gone down under the big, turning disks.

Which, like the tractor, did not care. The disks were doing only what they were told. They were turning. That was all and everything they were supposed to do. Turn. And turn. And turn.

Billy remembered Robert coming out behind. Coming out striped red and cut and pressed into the dirt. He did not get up. He was flattened and cut right into the field. And he kept getting smaller as the tractor kept rolling downfield.

For no one had told it to stop. Not Billy. He could not remember how to stop it. Finally he jumped. Let the tractor go. He leaped clear, into the soft dirt, and ran, screaming, back toward Robert.

Which was when his parents returned. It was one hour, nearly exactly, just like they said, when they drove back into the farmyard.

They saw Billy on the tractor.

They saw him leap.

They saw him running down the field and the tractor driving by itself and something crumpled in the dirt far behind. Billy's mother screamed and his father drove right through the barbed wire fence to get to the field.

But they were too late. One hour ago they had two sons. Now they had only one.

Later, at the hospital, in the basement, outside the room where Robert's body lay, the sheriff did his report. An accident report. It was part of his job, he explained. "And I have to ask one question," he said.

The three of them, Billy, Mavis and Abner, were white and silent. Staring, white and silent.

"I have to ask this," the sheriff said. "Who was driving?"

Abner slowly turned his head to Billy.

Who stared at his father.

Billy's mouth came open. He tried to speak.

But his father spoke first. His father's voice, both loud and far away, echoed inside Billy's head.

"I was driving," Abner said. "It was me."

one thing Billy Baggs had plenty of was work.

On this hot Saturday, the first one in August, Billy stood knee deep in a wagonload of corn and oats. It was Billy's job, while his father drank coffee with the men in the Feedmill office, to unload the wagon. With a scoop shovel he pushed the ears of corn and the pale oats. He made the grain pour yellow and white down through the square hole in the floor. A shiny iron grate covered the hole. Below the floor were large, humming grinders that crushed the corn and oats into a fine, white meal for his father's dairy cows. Billy tried to keep a steady avalanche going. The sooner he was finished, the sooner he could sit outside on the loading dock. Across from the Feedmill was the field where the town kids played baseball.

Shaking kernels of oats from his cuffs, Billy scraped the wagon bottom mostly clean with his boots, then headed to the front office. He stopped at the door to look through its dusty glass. Several men stood inside. Billy paused a moment, then opened the door.

A half dozen men, all dressed in dusty coveralls and caps, stood in the front office. Around them were shelves of farm supplies: seeds, insecticides, fertilizers; their smell always made Billy's nose itch. The men held white Styrofoam cups of coffee. A short man was saying, "So she answers, 'I've seen smaller, I've seen larger.'" The other men grinned expectantly. Among them, Billy's father, Abner Baggs, was tallest, dustiest, and wore the greasiest cap. He also had the most teeth missing.

"Done—" Billy said to his father. The short man stopped his joke. The others also turned to look. In the silence, outside the Feedmill, Billy heard the *ding!* of a bat, then faint cheering.

"Already?" Abner Baggs said. He was a lean man with long arms and darker hair than Billy's. Though Abner was tall, the top of Billy's yellow head was now nearly to his father's chin. Someday soon he would be able to look his father straight in the eyes. "You sure?"

"Yessir."

"Wagon corners swept out?"

"Yessir," Billy lied. Abner had a short leg and so would not climb into the wagon to look. Billy knew this. His father could not climb easily and he could not run. He could not catch Billy if he tried.

"Floor grate clean?"

"Yessir."

"It don't rain, we gonna need every kernel, you know."

The other men nodded.

"What if I checked your broom work?" his father said. He raised one dark eyebrow.

"Go ahead," Billy said. He raised his chin.

Abner winked at the other farmers, who chuckled. Billy felt his ears and neck grow warm. "All right, then," Abner said. He fished in his pocket, finally came up with a shiny dime. He tossed it to Billy. "Get yourself some peanuts, Son, and then wait outside."

Billy caught the dime without looking at it, then turned away. Son. The only time Abner said Son was in front of other people. So it didn't count.

He went to the little peanut machine by the door. It had a glass hopper full of dusty Spanish peanuts. He put in the dime and turned the handle. A small flood of red husks and brown meat fell into his hand.

"Anyway," the man who was telling the joke said, "so the man says . . ."

Billy shut the door behind him.

In the long warehouse filled with seed and feed, a flock of sparrows pecked at the floor. Billy threw the handful of peanuts to the birds; then he went outside to the sunlight and blue sky, and the sounds of boys playing baseball.

Billy sat on the loading dock and dangled his legs over the edge. Across the street and near the school was a park with tall elm trees. Alongside that was the baseball diamond. It had bright-green grass, reddish dirt for the base paths and infield and sharp white lines that held it all together.

The left-field fence was a curving row of colored signs. Gary's Welding. Emma's Café. Torvik John Deere. First Farmer's Bank. John's Plumbing & Cesspool. Flint Doctors' Clinic. Randy Meyers A-1 Cars.

And of course the players. The team in the field wore gray long pants with white socks and black stirrups. They wore red T-shirts and blue caps. Two players in black T-shirts and red caps held at first and second base. All of them waited, crouched.

On the mound the Flint pitcher lifted his leg, and his sleeve flashed. Billy, a half block away, saw the baseball, a faint streak of white. He heard the *ding!*

CHAPTER ONE
1970

Billy Baggs was thirteen and he had never played baseball. Never, that is, on a team with other boys. Never in uniform with black stirrups over white socks and a jersey with a number all his own. He had never even owned a real baseball glove or a Minnesota Twins cap. There were lots of nevers in Billy's life.

He never went to the movies.

He never went on vacation.

His family never had a new car.

"There ain't never enough money," his father always said.

The Nevers family. That should be their last name. He would be Billy Nevers.

But no one can choose his own name or his own family, just as no one can choose what he looks like. So he was Billy Baggs, a rangy, broad-shouldered boy with yellow hair, squinty blue eyes and crooked teeth. The Baggs family lived on a farm twenty miles from Flint, a town of 2,001 in northern Minnesota. And

The right fielder began to race toward the fence. Toward Billy.

A fly ball curved toward the fence, which was not far from the street in front of the Feedmill.

The right fielder made a running catch at the ball.

"All right!" Billy called. It just came out of his mouth. The right fielder, a kid about his own age, did not look around. He turned and fired the ball back toward the infield in time to hold the runners. Some parents clapped and cheered. The outfielder held up his fist. Then he looked over his shoulder at Billy. Billy wished he had not cheered.

The next batter came up. Billy leaned sideways to see better. Then he looked behind him, at the Feedmill office. The men were still talking. And in the back room, ears of corn still thumped in the grinder.

Billy looked up at the sun; it was high noon. Summer was more than half over. He was not sure how many more Saturdays the town boys would play. He looked back once more, then hopped down from the loading dock. He crossed the street.

At the edge of the park, just beyond the sidewalk, he stopped in the shadow of a tree and watched. This was the closest he had ever been to the field.

The players were all about his age. Some of them wore shiny leather shoes, real baseball shoes, with cleats. A few wore colored batting gloves, like the players on baseball cards. Billy had gloves. Right now in his hip pocket he carried worn cowhide farm gloves.

A big man with a large belly, wearing a small cap and holding a clipboard, stood beside the dugout. The coach. Billy recognized him from school, but could not remember the man's name. At school—next month he would be in eighth grade—Billy came and went unnoticed. He rode the Number 11 orange bus to school and rode it home. Because the Baggs farm was twenty miles from town, Billy was the first one to get on his school bus and the last one to get off. Because of the farm work and his chores, he had no time for sports after school. Not that he wanted to anyhow. He spit to the side.

Billy leaned against the tree and watched. Another fly ball lifted, this time to center field. "Get it!" Billy said.

The center fielder, a small boy, circled, finally reached up—and missed the ball completely. Base runners advanced. The center fielder picked up the ball and threw it toward the catcher's waiting glove; it was a weak throw far to the side. One runner scored.

"Come *on*, Tim!"

"Get it together, Tim!"

The shouts came from his own teammates. The stocky coach stepped forward from the dugout and stood with his hands on his hips. He was not looking at the little center fielder who had dropped the ball, but at the rest of the defense. "It's okay, Tim—we'll get it back. Now play ball out there."

Tim slapped his glove determinedly and got ready.

Billy watched two more batters strike out cleanly. The Flint pitcher was a strong right-hander who seemed to know all the moves.

Billy, a left-hander, was also a pitcher.

He had one old, brown baseball, and sometimes in the evening when his chores were done he pitched it against the side of the granary. On one board was a wide, dark knothole about knee high: that was his target, his catcher's glove. Some nights he could hit the dark spot, some nights he couldn't. Some nights he pretended he was playing catch with his brother, Robert, and then he threw straighter. They had played lots of catch. Robert had taught him. Robert had taught him everything. He was teaching Billy how to disk the day it happened.

On the field there was a sharp *ding!* The batter ran toward first base as the ball curved high toward right field. Toward Billy himself.

This time the right fielder ran to the fence but did not leap. The ball was over his glove, over the fence. It bounced on the sidewalk. Billy sprang away from his tree, raced and caught the bouncing ball.

There, in the middle of the street, he stared down at the ball in his hand. At its smooth whiteness. Its barely scuffed curves. Its unbroken threads. Its hard, raised stitching. He rolled the ball in his fingers.

"Give me the ball, kid!" the right fielder called.

Billy looked up quickly. The kid wore sunglasses that flipped down, and streaks of black greasepaint on his cheeks.

"You want a ball, buy one of your own," the kid said.

The players and the coach were looking out toward the fence, at Billy and the right fielder. The runner was trotting around third on his way home.

"Here's your ball," Billy said. He reared back and threw it.

His throw was flat and hard. The ball arced slightly over first base, then sank on a hard, straight line to home base. The catcher caught it with a loud *pop!* and tagged the startled runner.

There was immediate shouting from the players—all the players on both sides—and the parents as well. Of course the runner was safe; the ball was out of the park! There was a great hubbub at home plate.

In right field there was only silence. The right fielder with the sunglasses looked at Billy, then at home plate. His mouth hung open. Suddenly he turned his back on Billy and walked away. Back at home plate Billy saw the coach shading his eyes, looking.

Looking at Billy.

Who was now in double trouble.

Behind him, from the Feedmill, Billy heard the voice of his father, calling and calling his name.

CHAPTER TWO

"here the hell you been?" Abner said. He waited for Billy on the Feedmill dock. His elbows were winged out, his gloved hands on his hips. And he was dusty from loading bags of meal.

"I was just—"

"You was just what?"

"Across the street," Billy said. He hopped up onto the loading dock and grabbed a bag.

"I been callin' and callin'," Abner said. "You run off again, you ain't comin' to town next time."

"Then you'd have to unload the wagon yourself," Billy muttered.

"What's that?" Abner said.

"Nothin'," Billy said. He hoisted one of the heavy burlap bags and tossed it forward into their wagon. It lit with a puff of pale dust.

"It better be nothin'," Abner said, still glowering at Billy.

Billy worked on in silence.

After a while Abner looked across the street at the park. At the baseball field. "Some people sure got the life of Riley," he said, and spit.

Riley. Billy always wondered who Riley was. He didn't ask. There were lots of things he didn't ask his father, or anyone for that matter. He talked to Robert, but Robert never answered; he just listened. Robert in the shadows of the trees, Robert in the dark of night, listening.

"All summer the kids play ball. The parents take vacations. Damn lucky for them they's some people in the world who work," Abner said. He stood watching the baseball players as Billy tossed the one-hundred-pound sacks of meal. "Hell, I bet none a them over there, kids or adults, could lift one bag of feed."

Billy kept working. Each sack thudded into the wagon with a puff of dust. Each time, the wagon jolted and the springs squeaked.

"Though I used to play ball some," Abner said, in a softer voice.

Billy kept working but moved slower. He knew enough not to stop and stare at his father. Then Abner would clam up and turn things back to work. Slowly Billy kept moving the bags of meal.

"In the evenin'. After chores. Kittenball, that's what we called it. Me and my brothers had a stick and a big fat kittenball. Softball nowadays, I guess." Abner spit a long stream of brown tobacco juice toward the street. "Hell, I could throw that thing farther than any of them." He paused and stared off, beyond even the ballplayers. "Then I got polio."

Billy paused and looked sideways at his father.

Abner still stared across at the ball field. But he was not really looking at it. "I had two brothers. And there was the whole rest of the school. But it was just me and the Einarson boy, that summer of 1938. We was the only ones to get polio."

Billy stood upright and turned to his father. His mouth came open like he was going to say something. He didn't know what.

Abner turned and blinked. He saw Billy standing there, looking at him.

"But that's spilt milk, ain't it? Water over the dam."

Billy nodded.

"Hurry up with that feed," Abner said. "We got cows to feed at home."

Billy stooped for another bag as Abner limped inside to pay the bill.

When the cart was empty, Billy rolled it back into the Feedmill for the last load of bags. He waited by the big galvanized aluminum funnel where the ground meal came down. The miller pulled a lever and filled the last bag of the meal. He was dusty from cap to boots, a white dust mummy. Billy wondered how old the man was. Not that old, maybe a couple of years out of high school. But his eyebrows and the hair sticking out of his cap were snow white from the dust. Billy wondered what would it be like to work in a feedmill all his life. The dust in the nose. In the lungs.

Billy wondered what his own job would be. Where

he would work. The farm, he supposed. That was the only sure thing for him. The farm and the cows. There was always plenty of that work. He wondered what Robert would have turned out to be. What he would have done in life. Mavis, their mother, said Robert could read at age five. Billy hated reading. He was nearly fourteen and he still had to move his lips.

The miller tied off the last bag. A quick double wrap, with a short piece of twine, around the skinny neck of the bag. Then a quick movement of the miller's fingers—like a gambler's trick, too quick to figure out. Then a final upward jerk. Each bag of meal tied tight but not knotted. At home, one tug on the twine and the bag fell open.

"Bags for the Baggs family," the man said.

Billy said nothing. He was used to the jokes about his name.

"Hurry up, there," Abner called to Billy from the doorway, where he stood with some other farmers. "We ain't got time to stand around and talk."

The miller slowly rolled the bags onto the cart. "Your old man's in his usual good mood, I see," he said.

Billy glared. He didn't like the way the miller said it. "We got cows to feed."

"Like father, like son," the man said. Because of the dust on the miller's mustache, his eyebrows, Billy did not know if the miller was smiling.

"Just gimme the bags," Billy said.

"Suit yourself, kid."

Billy wheeled away the cart and the last load of

bags. He would be happy to get out of here and to be heading home. But as he wheeled the cart onto the loading dock, he braked to a stop. There, walking up to the Feedmill dock, was the baseball coach.

CHAPTER THREE

Billy's cart jerked to a stop, but the top sack of grain kept moving. It flew over the dock straight at the coach, who jumped to the side. The great sack *ploomp*ed right where the coach had been. A cloud of dust puffed upward and hung in the sunlight.

"I heard farming was a dangerous job," the coach said, waving his way through the dust. "Now I know for sure." He smiled at Billy.

Billy remained behind the cart, between its handles. For a big man the coach was as quick on his feet as a cat.

"What's going on here?" Abner said behind Billy. He stood in the doorway, holding the last of their supplies. Dust from the fallen bag floated and drifted in the sunlight.

"One of the bags—" Billy began.

"No problem," the coach said to Billy. He set his clipboard on the loading dock and squatted before the sack of grain. With a quick shrug upward, he flipped the heavy bag into the wagon.

Abner raised one eyebrow.

"Pay more attention to your work," Abner growled at Billy. "You'll hurt somebody and they'll sue us."

"Not me," the coach said.

"You never can tell nowadays," Abner replied.

Dusting off his hands, the coach turned to Billy. "You're the young fellow who picked up the home-run ball, aren't you?"

Billy nodded.

"Ball? What ball?" Abner said.

"When I was across the street. One came over the fence."

"He take one of your balls or something?" Abner said harshly. He caught Billy by the back of his shirt.

"No—not at all," the coach said.

Abner looked at the coach, then slowly released Billy.

"My name is Oswald Anderson. I teach at the middle school, and summers I coach baseball."

Abner nodded once but made no move to hold out his hand. "If there's no trouble, what do you need with my boy here?"

"It's not that he took the ball. It's how he gave it back," the coach said.

"What are you getting at?" Abner asked impatiently.

"Well," the coach said. He looked over his shoulder and pointed. "He threw it from the street, here, all the way to home plate."

Abner stared toward the field. "That don't look so far to me."

Coach Anderson turned back to face Abner. A small shine, the beginning of a smile, came to his eyes. "I'd say it's far enough."

"Well you got your ball back, that's the main thing, ain't it?" Abner said.

Billy began throwing bags into the wagon. The coach hopped lightly up onto the dock. "Give a hand?"

"He don't need any help," Abner said.

The coach was silent. He watched for a while. Then he said to Billy, "I guess I didn't get your name, son."

Billy looked sideways at his father, then back. "Billy. Billy Baggs."

The coach reached out his hand. "Oswald Anderson. Most people call me Coach."

Billy blushed and extended his hand. The coach's hands looked fat, but were thick and firm.

"Baggs," the coach said. "Eighth grade?"

"Going into eighth," Billy said

The coach surveyed his shoulders. His arms. "You ever think about playing summer baseball?"

"Some kids got to work in the summer," Billy said. He glanced sideways at Abner, who nodded his approval.

The coach was silent. He looked at the pickup, the wagonload of grain sacks. "Dairy?" he said to Abner.

"Maybe," Abner said, "though it could be hogs."

The coach's eyes fell on Abner's farm supplies. "Fly spray and teat wash. That says milk cows to me."

Abner pursed his lips. "We milk cows."

"How big's your herd?" the coach asked, like he was truly interested.

"Big enough for us," Abner answered. "Milk twenty. Forty head all together."

The coach nodded. "I don't know many people who could handle a dairy herd," he said. "Seven days a week."

"Feels like eight days, most weeks," Abner said with a sigh. Then his voice turned sharper, like he realized the coach was sweet-talking him. "And we ain't gettin' nothin' done standin' here." He eased himself down from the loading dock and took the rider's seat of the pickup. "Come on, Billy, we got to get on home."

Billy's eyes widened slightly. On the farm he drove everything, tractors and trucks alike, but he had never driven in town. He took the driver's seat. The wheel.

"You folks come to town every Saturday?" the coach asked. He leaned down to Abner's window.

"Most often," Abner said.

"Maybe next Saturday Billy could come over to the field, play a little ball."

Abner spit just to the side of Coach Anderson. "Naw. I don't think so. He might get to thinkin' he could take the summer off. Like some people."

The coach met Abner's gaze, then turned to Billy. "I could use a good outfielder. Of course he'd only be a backup," he added.

"Backup?" Abner said.

"I've got my first team pretty well set," Coach Anderson said. "The season's almost over. And besides, I've only seen Billy throw a ball once."

Abner glanced at Billy. "One throw's as good as the next."

"Maybe," the coach said. "Though how would I know?" He winked ever so slightly at Billy.

Abner snorted. "Start her up," he said to Billy. "Let's hit the road."

Carefully, in case the town policeman came by, Billy drove the pickup away from the Feedmill. The wagon trailed straight behind. In the rearview mirror, he saw the coach standing there with his clipboard, watching them. Growing smaller.

"Pretty smooth operator, that fella," Abner said. "You got to watch out for his type."

Billy was silent. He looked back to the baseball field.

"Keep your eyes on the road," Abner said.

Billy drove on, past the gas station, then turned toward the main highway.

"Now pull her over and stop," Abner said. "I'll take the wheel on the highway. Don't want to get us arrested."

Billy got out and went around to the rider's side. "So why'd you let me drive away from the Feedmill?" he said as they settled back in.

"Because the coach was there," Abner said.

Billy was silent.

"Farm kids is different," Abner said. "They know

how to do more things and so they got responsibility. Seemed like that coach needed a reminder." Abner waited, then pulled onto the highway in front of a shiny motor home, which braked suddenly and tooted its horn.

Abner drove at twenty-five miles per hour without looking back. Cars bunched up behind him, but he did not pull over or give way. Not Abner. Finally there was clear space ahead, and the big motor home passed them. There were bicycles and a short TV antenna on top, and a picture window in back. Three kids, two of them girls, all about Billy's age, lay on a mattress watching the highway recede behind them. They waved. Billy did not wave back. The girls made faces, then laughed hysterically and rolled out of sight. Beyond them was the mother, sitting with her feet up, reading a book.

"Life of Riley," Abner said, leaning backward in the seat. "Some people sure got it made."

Billy was silent.

"Take that Oswald Anderson fellow. The coach. A guy like that works nine months. Then has three months' paid vacation. He's got health insurance, every benefit you can think of, with a government job like that. But if he had to work for himself, why, he'd starve to death in six months."

"He can throw a sack of feed," Billy said.

Abner turned to stare at Billy, then looked back down the highway.

They rode another mile. "So what do you think?" Billy said.

"About what?"

"Next Saturday."

"What about it?" Abner said. He spit out his window, then looked down the road again.

"Me maybe bringin' my glove to town."

Abner was silent for a spell. "Backup outfielder," Abner muttered. "Who does that coach think we are?"

"Does that mean I can?" Billy said.

"I'll think on it," Abner said. "Next Saturday is a long way off. We might need cattle feed by then and we might not. It might be rainin'. Hell, we could be struck by lightnin' and burned crisper than your mother's pork chops by Saturday, so don't go gettin' your hopes up."

Billy showed no emotion. Nothing one way or another. He was good at that kind of look. Inside was another matter. He felt the wagon rolling behind, felt its weight pulling backward on the truck. But the truck had plenty of power. At this moment it knew what to do, and so did he. Once home he would unload the ground meal as quickly as possible so he could start feeding the cows. He had the feeling it was going to be their lucky week.

CHAPTER FOUR

The Baggs farm was three miles off the main highway. After asphalt the road was gravel, and the truck's tires threw up small stones that *ping-ting*ed in the wheel wells. Fine brown dust rolled up behind the wagon.

Billy and his father arrived at their driveway. It was marked, like all farms, by an aluminum mailbox in the shape of a little barn.

BAGGS, theirs read. The faded letters were hand-painted in black. Beneath, in smaller black letters, were ABNER, MAVIS and BILLY. Between MAVIS and BILLY was a rusted, empty space. One year to the day after Robert had died, Abner had taken down the box and sanded away his name.

Abner used a power sander. He spent over an hour sanding. It was at night, and the sparks flew from his grinder like a stream of fiery, falling stars. Billy heard him cursing and crying as he worked. Mavis made Billy stay out of sight.

Afterward Abner nailed the mailbox back onto the post and went to bed and slept. But he had sanded too hard, had sanded away the galvanizing. After the first rain, a spot of rust appeared where Bobby's name had been. The rust spot grew. Whenever it rained, the rust ran and bled down the post. One day, Mavis quietly mentioned that they could use a new mailbox.

"What's the matter with the one we got?" Abner asked sharply. "Tell me what's wrong with it."

"One that's a little bigger, that's all," Mavis said softly.

"Ours is plenty big enough," Abner said.

And Mavis did not bring up the subject again.

Actually they hardly needed a mailbox, then or now. The Baggs family had no newspaper or magazine subscriptions. They had no credit cards, so there were few monthly bills. They gave no money to church or to any organization. Today, however, a thick object was tied on top of the mailbox.

"Damn catalogue," Abner said to Billy. "Better get it. Your ma knows it's comin'."

Billy hopped out and retrieved a Sears, Roebuck catalogue.

"We ought to send it on back," Abner said, and spit out the window. "Catalogues just put ideas in people's head and then get 'em in debt."

Billy nodded obediently.

"Get people wantin' things they don't need. Buyin' things they can't pay for. In the least catalogues are a waste of paper," Abner said. He spit again and turned the pickup into their driveway. As the wagon jolted along, Billy sneaked a look at the catalogue. On its cover was a pretty woman with red hair wearing a summer dress. She sat on a white chair on a big green lawn. Behind her was a modern house full of windows. Billy stared at the house, then turned to the back pages.

Women's fashions—dresses, bathing suits, brassieres—flashed up at him as the pages fanned under his thumb, but today Billy was interested in one section only: sporting goods.

He braked at Ping-Pong equipment, a shiny green table for $129.

He scanned backyard swimming pools, $299 and up.

He inspected the "deluxe" stationary exercise bicycle. The woman on the machine was a blonde, dressed in a black leotard and pink headband. Her long tan legs were shiny with sweat. But the price was even more amazing than the girl: $199! Why, Billy wondered, would anyone pay that kind of money for a bicycle with one wheel?

Billy glanced at his father, who stared ahead while he worked a toothpick between his sharp jaws. How much, he wondered, of what his father said was true? Probably not half, even. Maybe only a little. But some things he said had to be true.

And there was another problem still. Some things, some ideas, might be true for Abner, but how could they be true for Billy? Billy was not his father. Well, he was half his father. So did that make the things his father said half true?

Billy looked back at the catalogue, which fell open to the baseball section.

Four pages of bats and gloves.

Real baseball gloves. Long, shaped leather fingers bound tightly together with rawhide lacing. Signed by famous players like Roger Maris and Pete Rose and Sandy Koufax. He wondered how the players had time to sign their names to each one.

Billy had a glove. Sort of. It was Abner's old mitt, which is what they called it in his day. He could not use Robert's because Robert was right-handed. Billy had found the mitt high up on a shelf in the garage. Mice had eaten away part of the thumb and one finger, and white stuffing bubbled out like old popcorn. Billy's mother helped him fix it. She pushed wads of quilt cotton in the holes, then stitched two pieces of buckskin over them. Running the needle through leather was difficult, and once she jabbed her finger badly. Several drops of blood stained the leather, and she sucked on her finger. "How am I going to type with holes in my fingers?" she said. But then she smiled quickly at Billy and put thimbles on her fingers.

When she was done, Billy rubbed brown shoe polish into the pale buckskin. After that he treated the whole glove with the mink oil that they used on the farm to keep their leather work boots soft. The old mitt softened considerably, and even shined a bit in spots. But not even Billy's mother could make a silk purse from a sow's ear.

The old glove was flat. There was no curved, pre-shaped "powerpocket." No tightly laced webbing. No "piston-packed" heel. Its fingers, thick and wide, were not stitched together but stuck up like the tail feathers of an old turkey. The center of the palm had a round, indented spot where the ball would stay at least briefly, but the ancient mitt was little better than an oversized man's work glove with stuffed fingers. Today Billy stared at the new leather baseball gloves.

Suddenly Skinner, their old black Labrador, was barking loudly, running alongside the pickup, snapping at the tires.

Billy blinked and looked up. He was home.

He stared. There was the windbreak that Abner had planted, spruce trees that curved like a wall around the farm. Inside it the narrow two-story farmhouse, gray with peeling paint. Beyond that the low red barn that also needed painting. The outbuildings, low sheds made from poles, boards and tarpaper. Abner had a small sawmill back toward the swamp, and Billy helped him haul logs and then saw them into boards. The half-round sides of the trees were called slabs, and made good firewood. Or, to Abner, slabs made plenty good enough wall boards for cattle sheds. As a result, the farm looked homemade. Looked shabby and run-down.

In the garden Billy's mother stood up. She was wearing her garden coveralls, and a red kerchief across her forehead. Her nose was sunburned and her chin was smudged with dirt. She held up a gloved hand in greeting; she always wore gloves since she had started typing practice.

Billy waved. He glanced down at the woman on

the catalogue cover. At her wide green lawn and its white wicker furniture. He looked up again. They had no lawn furniture; hell, they didn't even have a lawn. Theirs was patches of thin grass run down beneath tractor wheels and Caterpillar tracks. The truth was, Billy suddenly understood, they were poor.

So his father was right. He should take the catalogue to the burner barrel, drop it in and light a match; they could never afford the things in the catalogue. He took one last look at the baseball gloves. "Fifty dollars," he murmured.

"Say what?" Abner said.

Billy looked up quickly and bit his lip. "Nothin'."

Abner raised one eyebrow as he saw the catalogue page. At the baseball gloves.

Billy let the pages go shut. When the pickup stopped, he trotted across the garden and handed his mother the catalogue. Her blue eyes brightened. She took off her gloves and wiped her face, leaving a smear of dirt on her forehead. For long moments she stared at the woman on the cover.

"I met the baseball coach. At the Feedmill," Billy said.

"Yes?" Mavis said distractedly. She pulled her eyes from the catalogue. Billy told her about the coach. About—maybe—next Saturday.

"It's fine by me, Billy," she said, smoothing the hair away from Billy's forehead. Her eyes dropped once again to the glossy pages. "But you better not talk on about it. You know your father. . . ."

Billy nodded.

"Have yourself some lemonade and a fresh ginger snap," she said. "They're coolin' on the kitchen table."

"Can't. I got grain to unload," he said.

She looked up at him, then nodded absently as her eyes fell back to the catalogue pages. To the brightly colored dresses.

Billy found Abner in the granary. "I can unload," he said to Abner. "I'll do it."

Abner stared, then limped toward the house. Billy began to cart the heavy bags into the granary. He worked in the dim light, moving back and forth in his boots across the smooth, mouse-chewed boards. Dust settled on his arms and neck and eyebrows and nose, making him look just like the Feedmill man, but Billy was not thinking of that. No, he was somewhere else. Billy Baggs was in a baseball uniform with white socks and black stirrups, a baseball cap and a real glove, crouched on the green grass of the outfield. There was blue sky and white clouds and the *ding!* of a metal bat. He saw the shining white ball soar his way.

CHAPTER FIVE

On Monday Billy repaired the hay wagons. Soon Abner would begin cutting alfalfa. With any luck not on Thursday; that would mean hay to bale on Saturday. Billy looked up often to check the sky for clouds.

A hayrack had a board floor sixteen feet long, no sides, and a short wooden back. Some of the floorboards needed replacing. With a crowbar, Billy jacked out the nails and lifted the broken boards free. The old boards he saved. They could be sawn into firewood. Bent nails went into a can. Later he could pound them straight and use them again. He took new boards from a stack by the sawmill and measured them. He drew pencil lines with a carpenter's square. Then measured again. "Measure twice, saw once," Abner always said. That was true.

Then Billy used the electric circular saw. He ran its humming blade along the pencil lines. The steel teeth whined close by his fingers. Once he pushed the power saw too fast—the blade jerked backward: kickback. He looked up to see if Abner was watching. Luckily he wasn't. Billy set again to work, more carefully this time. A piney smell of sawdust rose around the hayrack. Yellow pine dust sprayed on his arms and legs and feet. After sawing, he fitted the new boards into place and pounded them home.

"You don't need three nails; two will do," Abner said in passing. "Nails cost money."

"Yessir," Billy said.

On Tuesday he fixed fence. There were cracked fence posts and loose wires along the corral. The cattle could smell the alfalfa in the hayfield. They leaned on the posts, stretching their necks between the wires as they tried to get a bite of fresh hay.

Billy loosened the barbed wire, sank new holes in the damp black dirt, then set in the new posts. One of the fence posts he remembered. It had an odd knothole and a slight curve. All the posts came from their own land. Every winter, when the swamp was frozen, Abner and Billy went out with a chainsaw and a long sled. They culled out the smaller trees that were shaded or losing out to larger pines close by. Then they topped each fallen tree. Limbed it. Cut it into seven-foot lengths. Last, with two-handled drawknives, they peeled off the bark.

Over the summer the posts dried. The next summer they were soaked in a tank of kerosene mixed with drain oil saved from the tractor. It was Abner's homemade wood preservative. But what kept the posts from rotting in the ground also made for messy work. As he hoisted the oily-smelling posts and tamped them into the ground, Billy's arms and face grew filthy. He could see one black streak down his nose. He wiped it with his wrist and kept working—until someone tapped him on the shoulder.

Billy jumped.

Gina Erickson stood there grinning at him. She was eleven years old, a pest from down the road. At least twice a week she rode her bike over to the Baggs farm to bother Billy. She had red hair, freckles on her nose and a gap between her front teeth. She was short but already had two little bumps under her T-shirt. Her sister, Heather, had just turned fifteen and had more than bumps. Billy looked down the road, but there was no Heather today.

Gina scrunched up her face. "You look like you been dipped in shit."

"I'm workin'. If you hadn't noticed," Billy said.

"I noticed," she said. "I notice everything."

Billy squinted at her, then turned back to his post.

"I noticed you looked for Heather."

Billy kept working.

"And I noticed you looked at my chest."

Billy spit. "There ain't nothin' there, so why would I look?"

"There is too," Gina said stubbornly. "And anyway, boys always look. That's the first thing they do, when a girl walks up—look at her chest."

"Says who?" Billy said. He kept tamping the soft dirt around the new fence post.

"Says Heather."

"She should know," Billy said.

"See?" Gina said, and giggled.

"Beat it," Billy said. "I got work to do and I don't need some ten-year-old botherin' me."

"I'm eleven. Almost twelve."

Billy gave her the silent treatment.

"So why don't you come swimmin' with me and Heather this afternoon?" Gina asked. "At River-bend."

"I got work to do."

Gina was silent for a while. "Heather's gonna be there."

"So?"

"So, she said it's a good day for tanning. She might take off her top."

"So?"

"So you should see hers."

"I have," Billy said, which was true.

"When?" Gina said immediately, and made a face.

"That's for me to know and you to find out."

Gina swore. For a kid she had the dirtiest mouth Billy had ever heard.

"Anyway, I get to see eighty of 'em a day," Billy said, "and feel 'em, too." He stood up and pointed to the dairy cows.

"Gawd—you're disgusting!" Gina said. She wheeled her old bike around and began to pedal away.

Billy laughed. He watched Gina rattle off down

the driveway, her red ponytail flopping on her back. "Tell Heather maybe," he called. "This weekend for sure."

Gina flipped back her middle finger in reply. Billy smiled. He thought for a long moment of Heather. Heather also had red hair. As he reattached the wires, he thought of her in the river floating on her back, the sun shining on the curves of her wet, white skin. He had seen her swimming that way more than once. And she didn't care.

Abner returned. "What'd that Erickson girl want?" he said. He threw down two more posts.

"Nothin'."

"That's good," Abner said. He paused to stare down at Billy. "You be careful with those girls. Their mother ain't around much, and the old man's gone for good. I hear they're pretty wild. Especially that older one."

Billy kept digging. He didn't look up.

"That's what I hear," Abner said.

"I wouldn't know," Billy said.

"Well, let's keep it that way," Abner said.

"Yessir."

Abner limped away, and Billy turned again to his work. To the last wire. He ran the wire but left the curved staples half nailed into the posts. Then he used the wire stretcher, a short length of rope on a double pulley, with a chain that clamped onto the barbed wire. He braced his legs against the corner post and slowly drew each wire banjo-string tight. While he worked, he thought of Heather.

"Get it good and tight," Abner called. "We don't want the heifers gettin' into the alfalfa."

"Yessir."

Billy kept working. He imagined Heather, sunning herself on a big rock at Riverbend. He imagined her standing up, then diving into the blue water.

On Wednesday Abner castrated bull calves. The wild little black-and-white Holstein bulls, born in the spring, were now eight weeks old and weighed 150 pounds. A dairy farm could have only one bull. More bulls would fight for breeding privileges. They fought so hard they either injured themselves or else were too pooped to mount a cow. Since Abner could not get around the pen quickly, Billy's job was to lasso the calves and pull them forward into the squeeze-chute. There Abner threw down a lever. Metal side gates closed and squeezed the little bull upright. But every calf found some way to buck and clang against the chute, and this one was no different. It scrambled and blatted and reared. "Hold him tighter, dammit!" Abner called.

Billy grabbed a short rope and cinched the calf's hind legs together. Then Abner was ready for the operation. From a bucket of hot soapy water he brought up the little knife. He made one quick slice in the scrotum. Then with a downward milking motion he squeezed through the cut the two shiny gray testicles, then cut their cord. He dropped the testicles into a pail. Beside the pen, two barn cats meowed hungrily. Last, Abner sprayed the floppy scrotum with BlueKote disinfectant. Billy released the gate.

Now a steer, the calf leaped away free and bounded to the farthest corner of the pen. It stood there hunched over, wide-eyed and blinking. Billy couldn't say he blamed the little fellow. But castration was a part of cattle raising and the farm. It had to be done.

When the last calf was finished, Billy carried the plastic pail of slippery gray testicles up to the hayloft. Usually too scared to come forward, today the barn cats sniffed the air and meowed loudly. On their bellies they crept, closer and closer. Billy was finally able to pet the wariest one of all, a big gray tom with a torn ear. Then he slung the contents of the pail across the straw. The cats leaped forward in a loud, caterwauling scramble and began to chew and slurp.

On Thursday morning they tuned up the hay mower, an old one with a single wheel in the rear and a seven-foot-long cutting sickle that stretched out to the side. The mower had been used a long time already before it came to the Baggs farm. Abner bought used implements at farm auctions. Dispersal sales, when a farmer was losing his land to the bank or to dry weather, were good bets. There farm machinery usually went cheap.

The Baggs farm had never had a farm implement that was new and brightly painted. There was no John Deere green. No Allis-Chalmers orange. A tall new tractor with a cab over the seat and air conditioning—that was probably Abner's dream, Billy imagined. Or maybe a bright red Massey-Ferguson swather, which cut the hay, crimped it between two rollers to let out the moisture, and laid the hay behind in a perfect swath.

Or maybe Abner had other dreams. Maybe, like Billy, he dreamed sometimes of Robert. Of Robert coming back. Of Robert just suddenly showing up one day for supper . . .

Abner cursed. "Look at those sections," he said as he slid out the sickle. Each little triangular section blade was about the size of Billy's hand; a row of twenty or so made up a sickle. "If you'd get those damn gopher mounds cleaned off this farm, we wouldn't have to buy new sections every year."

"I got traps out," Billy said. "I already caught forty-two."

"There's two hundred gophers on this farm."

"I only got ten traps."

"You turn in them forty-two for bounty yet?"

"No," Billy said. The township paid a bounty of fifty cents per gopher. Gopher trappers had to clip off the front feet as evidence, then bring them to the township board to collect the bounty. Billy was saving up his gopher feet. In truth he had caught seventy gophers, which meant thirty-five dollars.

"You ought to cash 'em in and buy some more traps," Abner said.

Billy was silent. He had other plans for the money. What, he didn't know. But it was his money.

They continued working on the sickle. Billy handed his father the tools, a hammer and cold chisel, to cut away the rivets. Then a new section and two rivets to hold it. *Ping, ping, ping* went Abner's ball-peen hammer on the anvil.

Billy thought of the *ding* of the aluminum baseball bats.

"Hold it steady," barked Abner. He slid a shiny new section into place, then began to pound the rivets flat.

Ping, ping, ping, ping.

Billy looked up at the sky. It was a clear, cloudless day. Good for baseball. Or swimming. He thought of Heather. And even, disgustingly, of Gina.

"I'm gonna cut hay this afternoon," Abner said, glancing upward as well. "That alfalfa ought to dry good today and tomorrow."

Billy was silent. He scanned the sky, searching, hoping for clouds.

Ping, ping, ping.

On Friday morning they readied the hay baler. The weather held hot and dry. Twenty acres of alfalfa lay in windrows in the bright sunlight and breeze. With a grease gun Billy crawled slowly under and around the baler. "Get that grease fitting underneath the main auger," Abner said.

"Already did," Billy said.

"Did it take?" Abner asked.

"Took," Billy said sharply.

"Well, give it another shot," Abner said.

Billy bit his lower lip. He found the fitting and jacked in purple grease until it curled out in a large glob.

After greasing the baler they checked the big plunger, an arm with a square fist that punched the hay forward, compressing it in the long, square chamber. The plunger slid easily backward and forward. "Got to make sure it's aligned right," Abner said.

Otherwise it'll tear up the chamber. Billy waited for him to say it.

"Otherwise it'll tear up the chamber," Abner said. Then he looked inside the twine box.

Better get another bale.

"Better get another bale," Abner said to Billy.

Billy produced two fresh bales, yellow-orange spools of twine each about the size of a basketball. The twine was made in Brazil. As he cut open the packages it gave off a sharp, chemical smell, which kept mice and insects from chewing on the twine.

Abner checked the twine knotter and then the needles, two long, thin arms that speared the twine upward at the end of the bale. The knotter grabbed the twine and cinched it tight. Abner spliced the twine. He tied the leading end of the new twine onto the trailing end of the old spool, with a special knot that looped right-over-left, then left-over-right. A square knot. Then he rolled the knot briskly between his hands.

You got to smooth out the knot, else it won't pass through the needles.

"You got to smooth out the knot, else it won't pass through the needles," Abner said to Billy.

Billy looked away.

"There," Abner said, dropping the twine-box lid. "She's ready. Now let's hope it don't rain."

Billy took a breath. "Saturday. What about Saturday?"

"What about it?" Abner said.

"We're pretty low on cattle feed."

"I looked. There's enough to get us through till Monday or Tuesday."

Billy looked away. Off to the horizon.

At sundown the sky carried clouds. A faint line of them lay like a gray string laid across the west sky. Scattered thunderstorms were forecast, though only with a ten-percent chance in the area of the Baggs farm. Billy crossed his fingers and spit three times for good luck.

Much later, when he was in bed, he heard his parents' voices.

"It would mean a lot to him," Mavis said.

"Baseball or six hundred bales of hay," Abner said sharply. "I don't see no contest there."

"Look at all he's done this week," she said.

"Just a regular week of work on the farm," Abner said.

There was silence for a while. "He's only thirteen. You work him like he's a man, a full-grown man."

"Which will give him a head start on bein' one," Abner said. "It ain't never too early to work hard. That way he won't get funny ideas about the world. Like it's easy or somethin'. Like it won't try to knock you down."

Billy knew what he was talking about: Robert.

Billy's mother was silent. They did not talk about Robert. Ever.

"Besides, who else is gonna help me buck bales?" Abner said. "We can't afford to go out and pay nobody."

"I'll do it," Mavis said loudly.

Abner was silent.

"I might as well. That's what I feel like around here sometimes, just a hired hand."

Billy held his breath.

There was silence for long moments.

"If we can't bale hay, we'll go to town and he can bring his mitt," Abner said. "If the weather holds clear and dry, we bale."

And there was no more talk downstairs after that.

Billy lay in the dark in his bedroom under the eaves. Mosquitoes hummed outside his screen. He wondered sometimes what it was like to be married to someone. What that was like. On the one hand it meant that people had to be together all the time, even when they had arguments.

On the other hand it meant two people could do anything they wanted to. With each other, that was. Like take off their clothes and lie in bed together and do it. He was not sure if his parents still did it or not. He had the feeling that when Robert died a lot of things like that had changed.

Billy turned over in bed and tried to fall asleep in another position. He closed his eyes and saw the rat. Not a real rat. But real enough. It always came out of some hole in his mind when he was tired and sad. He could expect it then. Its sharp, pointy nose. Its whiskers that twitched and sniffed the air. Its beady black eyes. Its whole head turning toward Billy, looking straight at him. Accusing him.

Billy opened his eyes. The rat went away, but never all the way, just out of sight.

Suddenly, below in the kitchen, his father's fist pounded on the table. Pounded once—then again—on the wooden kitchen table. Billy lay there waiting for their argument to start up again. He didn't mind; at least the rat would stay away.

The pounding came again.

But the sound was wrong.

He listened closer. There were no voices downstairs.

Billy leaped from bed and crouched at his little window. Far off, in the west, were faint yellow fishhooks of lightning, then the thumping sound. Even as he listened, rain began to patter on the shingles. Rain!

In the dark bedroom he took the outfielder's crouch. "It's a high fly ball driftin' toward Billy Baggs," he whispered.

CHAPTER SIX

At breakfast Abner glared out the window at the gray clouds. "Be no balin' today," he muttered.

Billy sneaked a look at Mavis. She winked at him.

"Well, it didn't rain much," she said cheerfully. "Count your blessings."

"Some luck," Abner said, reaching for another pancake. "Just enough rain to wet the hay. Not enough to do the oats and corn a lick of good."

Billy said, "I might as well load up the wagon."

Abner peered out the window once again. "I suppose so," he said.

Billy wolfed down the last of his pancakes and bolted for the door.

"Hey," his mother called. "I've got more cakes on the griddle!"

The Baggs family, in their old Ford pickup, with the wagon hitched behind, arrived at the Feedmill at ten o'clock. Billy had loaded the grain in record time, but already there were several wagons in line ahead of them.

"Damn and double-damn," Abner said, surveying the other trucks. "It'll take us all mornin' to get out of here."

Mavis nudged Billy with her knee. "Well, I've got quite a few errands to run uptown," she said. Billy noticed that she had worn a nice dress today, her good one, blue with white squares. "Billy can go over to the ball field for a while," she added, "unless you need him for something."

Billy touched the old leather mitt inside his shirt.

Abner frowned briefly at Billy, then looked up at the Feedmill office where a cluster of men sat drinking coffee. "Naw, I guess I don't. But don't you forget the time," Abner added.

"I won't," Billy said.

"And remember who you are," Abner said.

Billy met his father's gaze for a long moment, then turned away. To baseball and the town kids.

Leaving his dusty farm cap in the truck, Billy crossed the street. He wore patched blue jeans, a work shirt with the sleeves cut off and low-cut Converse tennis shoes that Mavis had bought at a farm auction, from the junk table. They were a size too big; better that way than too small, Abner said. But Billy wasn't thinking about any of that.

Two lines of boys tossed balls back and forth. There were exactly the right number for pairs. No leftover kids. Billy recognized only one boy, Shawn Howenstein, the butcher's son.

Coach Anderson leaned against the dugout, watching his players. "Throw over the top, King," he called. "No fancy sidearm stuff."

Billy stopped among the big trees.

"Don't worry about speed, Jake," the coach called. "Just hit the target."

On the far side two pitchers, one right-handed, the other left-, threw to two catchers. Coach Anderson looked away from his pitchers toward the park. He noticed a boy leaning against a tree, watching the pitchers. It was the farm kid, Billy Baggs.

The coach raised his hand and waved.

For a moment Billy thought of ducking behind the tree, then heading back to the Feedmill. There he knew everything. Every bag of meal, every block of salt or fertilizer, every cart and tool, even the miller he knew.

"Hey there, Billy Baggs!" the coach called, and trotted forward.

Billy swallowed and stepped forward. He met the coach halfway.

"I was wondering if you'd show up today," Coach Anderson said. "Put it here!" He held out his hand.

Billy blushed and shook hands.

"You're just in time," the coach said. A slight pulling motion at the end of their handshake moved Billy forward, toward the other boys on the field. "A little rain last night, but the infield is still solid," the coach said. "Did it rain out your way?"

"Just enough," Billy said.

"Good, good." The coach talked easily, filling up Billy's silences.

They drew near the other boys. "Got a glove, I see," the coach said

"Sort of," Billy said. He held it up.

"Now there's a good old classic," the coach said, taking the glove. "Don't see many of these anymore." He tried it on. "It's good and solid." He smacked it several times with a fist. "This kind was mainly used for softball," the coach said. "You might want to think about a new one someday."

Billy turned around, looking briefly at the Feed-mill.

"But this one will do fine for right now," the coach added quickly. "You're used to it, and that's the important thing."

Billy nodded.

"You got a cap?" the coach said.

"Forgot it," Billy said.

"Let's head to the dugout. I think I got an extra one. Plus we'll get you signed up. You had a physical?"

Billy stared.

"A physical exam? By a doctor?"

Billy shook his head "No."

"Well, we can work around that for now," the coach said.

As they walked toward the dugout, several kids turned to look at Billy.

"Who's that?" someone said.

"Beats me."

"Looks like Huck Finn," a third kid called out.

The others laughed.

The pitcher, Archer "King" Kenwood, did not. He ignored Billy. He threw the ball smoothly, making it pop in the catcher's glove.

In the dugout Billy looked around. At the rack for bats. At the wire screen that deflected foul balls. At the long duffel bags of equipment. And at the wall. On a brown corkboard was pinned a fat stack of small papers. Above them was a note: "City Recreation League paid receipts here." "No pay, no play," someone had scrawled just below.

Twenty dollars.

Billy's shoulders stiffened.

The coach rummaged in his bag, then turned and tossed Billy a cap.

Staring at the rules, at the receipts, Billy missed it. The cap fell to the floor.

"Don't worry about the money," the coach said. He picked up the cap. "Anyway, the season's more than half over."

"So I should pay for what's left, then." Billy said. He felt his father's blood rise up in him, heard his father's voice in his own words. It was a kind of stubbornness, a hardness. "Ten dollars."

"Let's say eight," the coach said. "Eight dollars is fine. The cap is free. And then there's the game uniform. They're another ten dollars."

Billy turned and began to walk away.

The coach looked up. "Hey—where're you going?" He held out the cap.

Billy paused. "I . . . got to go. I gotta get back to the Feedmill."

"Wait." The coach caught up with Billy. "You don't have to pay today."

Billy shrugged.

The coach stared. "You're saying you don't have eighteen dollars, is that it?"

"I got it," Billy said. He looked back at the Feed-mill.

"But your father won't let you spend it on base-ball."

Billy turned back to the coach.

The coach nodded. "Okay, I see." He scratched his head. "Listen—I've got an idea. You can do some work for me. We'll figure something out. But later, okay? Right now I've got a practice to run."

"I should know—" Billy said.

"Know what?" the coach said, exasperated.

"How I can work out the eighteen dollars."

"I've got some . . . painting. At home. The trim on my garage," the coach said. He put the cap on Billy's head, pulled it tight on his forehead.

"I can paint," Billy said, smiling.

The coach looked down at him, this skinny, bony-shouldered, long-armed kid with the shock of yellow hair and crooked teeth, who smelled more than a little like a cow barn. The coach saw all kinds of kids in his job as teacher and coach. Often he wondered how they made it in life. Some kids had everything going for them, and some kids, like this Billy Baggs, had noth-ing. But most of them survived. Somehow they survived, and some of them did things with their lives he never imagined they would. That was the miracle. That was the payoff. "I'll bet you can paint," the coach said. "But right now get your butt out onto the field."

At first Coach Anderson played catch with Billy. "Easy does it!" he called on the first throw. "Just toss it soft to begin with."

Billy nodded.

He had to catch the coach's throws with two hands, with a clapping motion that trapped the ball, because his mitt had no real pocket.

"Great glove," whispered the boy next to him.

"What say, Nix?" called the coach.

"I said 'great catch,'" Doug Nixon said quickly.

"That's what I thought," Coach Anderson said, drilling the ball into Billy's glove. "But why don't you take two laps just in case I misheard you."

Nix muttered something, then turned away to take his laps.

"Billy—take over Doug's spot," the coach called. Before turning away to check on his pitchers he shouted out, "Boys—this is Billy Baggs."

The balls zipping between the two lines of players stopped moving as the boys inspected Billy. Then, slowly, balls began to lob back and forth again.

"Billy Baggs," King Kenwood said, too quietly for the coach to hear him. "Great name for a ballplayer."

Several other boys giggled.

"No, really," King said. The others thought about

that for a moment. King started throwing again and so did they. "But every ballplayer has a nickname," he added. "So what's yours?"

"Billy. Just Billy," Billy said.

"No way!" King said. "What do you think, guys, how about a nickname?"

They all turned to look at Billy. Look him up and down.

"Patched pants, no spikes," King said. "Looks kind of *ragged* to me."

"Rag Baggs!" someone shouted.

Billy dropped his glove and started toward King.

Coach Anderson caught him from behind. "Whoa; easy, boys," he said.

Billy and King stared at each other.

"You two need to get to know each other better. Why don't you play a little catch?"

"Sure," King Kenwood said.

Billy shrugged and picked up his glove.

They stepped off twenty paces and began. King threw straight and medium hard. Billy matched his throw.

When King threw chest high, Billy threw chest high.

When King threw left, Billy threw left.

When King threw low, Billy threw low.

As soon as Coach Anderson wandered off, King threw a ball that came straight—and curved down and in. The ball bounced off Billy's glove and rolled away.

King waited, whistling like he was bored, while Billy retrieved it.

"I know," King said as Billy got back into position. "Let's play killer catch."

Billy stared.

"It's a game," King said. "It goes like this. We each have a ball. We throw it to each other at the same time. That way we can play double catch. First one to throw a bad pitch or drop the ball is dead."

Billy shrugged. He caught the second ball tossed his way.

"Ready?" King said.

Billy nodded.

They both tossed their balls.

Both made the catch.

Both tossed. Both caught.

"See? Nothing to it," King said. He increased the speed slightly on his next throw.

Billy did the same.

Both threw. Both caught.

Gradually their speed increased. The other boys gave up their own throws and, pair by pair, turned to watch.

Billy was at a slight handicap with his two-handed catches, but made up for it with a quick release on his throw.

The balls began to flash in midair, white blurs that crossed exactly halfway between the two boys.

King began to grunt with the effort of each throw.

The balls popped louder and louder in their gloves.

Gradually Billy's balls began to reach the halfway point first.

King Kenwood, falling behind, began to catch

Billy's throws even as he released his own. King leaned into his throws. He was dangerously close to getting hit. But he would not give in.

Thunk-ow!! Billy's throw caught King squarely on the side of his shoulder, and the other ball popped free from King's glove. Both balls trickled to a stop by King's feet.

"Uhhhh." King bit his lip and squinted at Billy as he rubbed his shoulder. He looked around for the coach, and seemed about to take a step forward toward Billy.

Which was fine by Billy.

But Coach Anderson stood leaning against the dugout. He had been watching all the time. "Good warm-up boys," he called. "Now let's play ball."

CHAPTER SEVEN

Under gray skies the baseball team took fielding practice. If the weather held, later in the morning they would scrimmage. Their regular Saturday away game against the Buckman Warriors, the Flint Sparks' archrivals in all sports, had been canceled because of heavy rains there.

To Billy Baggs, jogging into the damp right field, the weather was perfect. On the farm, rainy days were holidays. Rainy days were for listening to the radio or sleeping or, more likely, coming to town. Rainy days were happy days. No farmer, not even Abner, could work in the rain. Billy smacked his old leather mitt with his right fist.

Tim Loren, the shrimpy outfielder, ran up beside him. "You right field?"

Billy nodded.

"Me too. In right field I can do the least amount of damage to the team," Tim said. His laugh, a high-pitched giggling, was like a girl's.

Billy took his place several paces behind the two

other right fielders. He wanted to be last so he could see how things worked. Tim trotted behind him.

"I get to be last," Tim said. "I'm always last."

Billy shrugged and tried to concentrate on the fielding practice. The coach stood to the side of home plate and hit balls that he tossed up himself. King Kenwood pitched to a nearby catcher. This made the coach's hits look like they were from a real batter.

"I like being last," Tim said. "You too?"

Billy ignored him. At first base, second, and all the other positions were short lines of players. It looked like each player would get one turn to field the ball and then throw in to home plate. When the coach was done with all the first basemen, he would turn to second base. Then to shortstop. And so on, to the outfield.

"What grade you in?" Tim asked.

"Eighth. Going into," Billy said. He stared toward home plate, and the coach.

"Me too," Tim said.

Coach Anderson *ding*ed the first ball toward first base. The player made a good catch and a sharp throw home.

"Next!" the coach called.

"Are you fourteen?"

Billy shook his head.

"Fifteen?"

Billy turned to glare at this kid.

"You can't be thirteen."

"Why can't I?"

"When's your birthday?" the pest asked.

"September. I'll be fourteen." Billy tried to keep his eyes on the coach.

"I turned fourteen in January," Tim said. "I'm shrimpy for my age. My nickname is Tiny. Get it?"

Billy shrugged.

"Tiny Tim."

Billy spit to the side.

So did Tiny Tim. "Some of the guys going into eighth grade are fifteen or even older," he said. "Like King and Nix."

Billy stared. Nix headed the left fielder's line. King was on the mound, pitching to a second catcher.

"Their parents held them back a year, at kindergarten."

"Why?" Billy said. "Are they retarded or something?"

Tiny Tim collapsed with laughter on the grass. "Retarded! That's rich, so rich—" he managed to say.

Billy ignored Tiny Tim.

"So they would be the biggest and best at sports in their grade," Tim said, recovering. "That's why. Lots of parents do that."

Billy shrugged.

"What about your parents?" Tim said.

Billy was silent.

"Your parents. What do they do?"

"Farm," Billy said.

Tim nodded. "What do they look like?"

Billy turned to stare at Tim.

53

"Look like," Tim repeated. "What do your parents look like?"

"I dunno," Billy said, turning away. "Just . . . regular."

"Tall or short?"

"Tall," Billy said, exasperated. "Brown hair." Some luck to get stuck next to this kid. He concentrated on the action at home plate.

"My parents are on vacation," Tim said, stooping to pick a blade of grass.

Billy was silent. He thought of the motor home.

"My sister and I didn't go along because we have school during the year and then stuff like baseball in the summer."

Billy turned. "How long have they been on vacation?"

Tim looked off toward home plate. "Five years."

Billy's mouth fell open. "Five years?"

"Since I was eight," Tim said.

"So who . . . Where do you live?"

"With my grandmother."

"Well, when are they coming back? Your parents?"

"Oh, very soon—" Tim said, turning to Billy and nodding confidently. "Very soon." He looked toward the street where a white car passed. "They could be back any day."

Billy turned his attention back to home plate. He wished he was playing near somebody else. He did not like this kid.

Tim was chattering again. "I don't mind living with Granny. She couldn't hear a cherry bomb if it went off in the kitchen. And she goes to bed at eight thirty every night. Plus she gives me all the money I want. I just have to ask for it," he said. He imitated an old woman's voice, "'It's really your money, dear,'" Tim quavered.

Billy concentrated on the field. Tried not to look at Tiny Tim.

"You don't believe me?" Tim said. "Look." He pulled a wad of green bills from his pocket. He peeled one off the roll. "Here—take one," he said. He stepped closer to Billy, held it out.

It was a ten-dollar bill. "No," Billy said. "I don't want your damn money."

"So I don't want it either," Tim said.

Billy watched, amazed, as Tim took off his baseball glove, then tore the ten-dollar bill into small pieces. Billy's eyes widened.

"I told you so, see?" Tim said. He threw the pieces into the air and let the breeze flutter them away, then grinned at Billy.

Something about his grin made Billy step away from this kid. He focused his eyes on the ball bouncing to second base.

Tiny Tim came up close to Billy. "So you want to come over some time? I've got two thousand nine hundred eighty-two baseball cards."

"Can't," Billy said.

"How about today?" Tim said.

Billy shook his head. "I never stay in town. Too

many crazy people in town."

"Please?" Tim said.

"No."

"Someday, huh? Please?"

Tiny Tim Loren was like a summer horsefly that kept buzzing and buzzing around Billy's head, trying to light on his hair and burrow in. How could he get free of this pest? "Maybe. Someday," Billy mumbled.

Tiny Tim grinned. "All right!" he said.

"Someday in the next century," Billy added under his breath.

"Okay, outfield—ready?" the coach called.

The coach tossed up a ball and cracked a high fly ball to left field. The left fielder trotted a few steps to his right, made the easy catch, then looped the ball into home plate.

"The runner scored on that throw," the coach called. "Put something on it next time."

The coach continued with the left fielders, then called, "Center!"

Already Billy was nervous. He swallowed. His mouth went dry and sticky.

Tiny Tim talked on about this and that, about girls at the town beach, something about a dressing room, but Billy hardly heard a word. Soon enough the coach called, "Ready in right!"

The first right fielder made a good catch and straight throw that bounced twice, slowing, on its way home.

The second right fielder trotted to his left to make the catch. He tried to make it look too easy—and dropped the ball.

"E-nine!" the coach called. "Concentrate!" He picked up another ball. "Ready out there, Baggs?"

Billy's legs felt shaky as he crouched. He felt eyes around the field boring into him. He felt like he couldn't breathe. Then there was the *ding!* of the bat, and the ball soared high into left center. Billy raced over, made a running, basket-style catch. Without coming to a full stop, he fired the ball to home plate. The ball soared on a rising arc over second base, over the pitcher's mound, over home base and even over the backstop. Billy stared. He had thrown the ball clear out of the park.

The coach watched the ball bounce down the street. Then he turned back to the outfield. "Nice catch, Baggs."

There was laughter and hooting. Billy's neck and cheeks burned hotly. He trotted back to right field.

"Ready, Tim?" The coach's bat *ding*ed and Tim ran forward. He waited—then ran backward—then changed his mind and came forward. The ball dropped just behind him. Several players groaned. With his short arm, Tim pegged the ball back to the infield. It bounced several times and trickled in to home plate.

"Nice recovery, Tim," the coach called, and waved everyone in.

"He always says that," Tim said to Billy. "'Nice recovery.'"

"Least you got it to home plate," Billy said.

"Actually I hate baseball," Tim said as they trotted toward the infield.

Billy looked at him. "So why do you play?"

"My shrink says I have to play."

"Your what?" Billy said.

"My shrink. My psychiatrist," Tim said. He grinned at Billy and bugged out his eyes. "I'm supposed to be crazy; can't you tell?"

CHAPTER EIGHT

The gray clouds lightened, and the players counted off by twos for the scrimmage. Billy noticed that King Kenwood and Nix Nixon made sure not to stand beside one another. And of course Tiny Tim Loren made sure not to stand beside Billy.

Tim tried to get King's attention about something. "See, King? See?" King nodded without even a glance at Tim. Billy thought of a little runty calf he'd once had on the farm. Its mother had died, and the calf followed anybody who came near, bawling and bumping against him.

"Okay." The coach finished some scribbling on his clipboard. "Ones are in the field. Twos at bat."

Billy was a two.

King Kenwood was a one. He took the mound. He was taller, an inch or more, than Billy. Though Billy had broader shoulders and longer arms, King was thicker through his chest and thighs. He stood at the mound scraping the red dirt here and there like he knew exactly what he wanted.

Billy sat in the far end of the dugout. Tiny Tim sat next to him. They watched King throw his first warm-up pitch, with a smooth motion. It flew straight in for a strike.

"His big brother teaches him everything," Tim said. "He pitches for the minor leagues, Triple A ball."

"Sure," Billy muttered.

"Really!" Tim said. "For the San Francisco Giants."

"Right."

"Ask anybody," Tim said.

The next pitch was faster, and also right on target. King did not look at anyone else except the catcher as he threw again, still harder. The ball popped in the catcher's glove. King's motion—the smooth back step, the swinging arms, then the forward stride and follow-through—was exactly the same each time. It was natural-looking, like he had been pitching all his life.

Tim chattered on about King's brother, Dick Kenwood. Where he pitched in college. When he was drafted by the Giants. His stats in the minors. Then the coach's voice echoed in the dugout. "Leading off is Tim Loren."

"Huh?" Tim said. His eyes bugged out for real.

"Let's go, Tim!" the other boys shouted. There was laughter.

Tim clutched Billy's arm. "I can't," he whispered to Billy. "I never hit the ball!"

"Get out there," Billy said.

Tim just sat.

"Or else I'll boot you out there," Billy added.

Tim gave Billy a hurt look and stood up. He walked slowly toward the bat rack. He chose the shortest bat and dragged it toward home plate.

"Okay, Tim," the coach called. "Let's hear it in the dugout," he said quietly.

There was weak cheering for Tiny Tim.

"Eyes open all the time," the coach said. "Remember what Pete Rose says: 'See the ball, hit the ball.'"

"Pete Rose gets two hundred hits a season—I've never had one," Tim said.

There was laughter from both the dugout and the field. The good kind of laughter.

Tim stepped up to the plate.

"Halfspeed?" King Kenwood asked Coach Anderson.

"You guys decide," Coach Anderson said.

"Yes, halfspeed," Tim said. Then he looked back to the dugout. At Billy. "No," Tim said. "Full speed today."

"You sure?" King said.

Tim swallowed, then nodded.

"Okay," King said, in an it's-your-funeral tone.

Tim stepped just inside the batter's box and planted himself there. He touched his stubby bat to the inside of the plate.

"Step in closer," the coach advised. "You've got to protect the outside corner."

Tim eased a half step closer and crouched over very low.

"Hey—he can't do that!" King called, straightening up and stepping off the pitching rubber.

"Balk!" someone called from Billy's dugout.

"Why not?" the coach asked King.

"He's got a four-inch strike zone."

"So practice your control," the coach said.

King smacked the ball into his glove several times, then leaned down for the sign. He wound up and threw.

With his eyes squinted tightly shut, Tim swung wildly at the ball.

"Strike one," said the coach, who was also the umpire today. "Remember—eyes open."

Tim nodded. Peeking out from under his cap he watched, frozen, as the next two pitches sailed past. Both were high.

"Two and one," the coach called.

"Be oh and three on anybody except a midget," King muttered.

"Pitch the ball," the coach said.

On the next pitch, Tim squinted and swung—and fouled it back into the screen.

There were cheers. Tim looked back in wonder. "I hit it!" he shouted, "I actually hit it!"

"Nice contact," the coach said.

King Kenwood wound up and threw again. High this time.

"Full count."

Shaking his head, King paused to rub up the ball.

Then he readied himself for the next pitch.

Tim, realizing King Kenwood was not happy, stared in panic at the mound.

"Get ready," the coach said to Tim. "Swing!"

Tim jammed his eyes shut and flailed at the ball. There was a soft rap, and the ball skidded weakly down the third baseline.

"Run!" the players screamed at Tim from the dugout. "Run!"

Tiny Tim opened his eyes—then sprinted toward first base.

Both the third baseman and King Kenwood raced toward the ball, which trickled along the white stripe of the baseline. It appeared to be rolling foul. At the last moment, King waved off the third baseman, and the two of them let the ball roll.

It stopped dead just at the edge of the line. "Foul ball," King called, and went to pick up the ball.

"Wait!" Coach Anderson said as he jogged toward them. The third baseman shrugged. By now Tim stood on first base.

Coach Anderson knelt down by the ball. Players in the dugout rushed out to see better. The coach peered at the ball, then lay all the way down on the red dirt.

Tiny Tim's whole team lay down. They all lay on the ground, eyes level with the ball and the foul line.

The coach stood up and slowly dusted off his pants. He looked at the expectant boys. "Base hit!" he called.

Billy's team jumped and cheered wildly. Tiny Tim hopped up and down on first base like it was a trampoline. King Kenwood turned to glare out across center field.

"Batter up," the coach called, chuckling to himself. The players filed back into the dugout. Billy sat down and waited. Nobody came to the plate.

"Batter?" the coach called.

Someone jumped up to look at the clipboard on the wall, where the lineup was listed.

"Baggs!"

"Head in the game, Baggs!" the coach called. Billy leaped forward and grabbed a bat—any bat—and rushed to the plate.

"Always check the lineup card," the coach said.

"Right," Billy said, his cheeks red with embarrassment.

"Batting helmet!" several of his teammates called. Billy looked around.

"Here," the coach said, handing Billy a blue helmet. Billy pulled it on. His head suddenly felt oversized; sounds echoed inside the helmet's dome. He felt like he was wearing a milking pail.

"Fit all right?"

Billy nodded.

"Okay, now you're ready," the coach said.

Billy stepped into the batter's box.

"Easy out," the third baseman called.

"Bottom of the order bats first today," someone else called.

Inside the white line of the batter's box, Billy's feet went into the grooves that every player used. He touched his bat to the hard rubber plate. It looked very large. Billy wondered how wide home plate was; he had never thought of that before. Its hard rubber was cut and sliced by cleat marks, and Billy touched it with the end of his bat. The aluminum bat felt long and light in his hands. Its rubber-sleeved handle was soft and sticky in his palms. Without any practice swings he readied himself for the pitch.

Which sent him stumbling backward. A high, inside fastball almost hit him.

"Stay in there," the coach said. "That was a brushback. Ball one."

Billy crouched closer to the plate this time.

King Kenwood wound up and threw hard and inside again.

Billy lifted only his chin as the ball whistled by and smacked into the catcher's glove.

"Ball two."

Billy waited for the third pitch. It was low and on the outside corner, and Billy took a rip at it. But the ball was inches off the end of his bat.

The coach trotted around the catcher and put his hands on Billy's hips. "Stride straight ahead—at the pitcher. You're stepping out with your lead foot. That leaves the outside corner unprotected. Try it."

Billy took a couple of practice strides straight forward. Then he nodded and stepped back into the box.

"Two and one," the coach called.

Billy watched the next pitch sail straight at the center of the plate. He lunged forward and took a mighty swing. The bat went *ting* and the ball sailed high and foul. King Kenwood stared up at the ball.

"Don't try to kill it," the coach said to Billy. "Two and two."

Billy readied himself.

King Kenwood wound up, then threw.

Billy, swinging way too soon at this one, stumbled forward. The ball came in a lot slower than before. It floated toward the plate. Billy managed to get just a piece of the ball. It squirted hard off the end of his bat and down the first baseline, foul.

"Watch out for the change in speeds," the coach said. "Try to keep your weight back."

Billy nodded and dug in. He leaned more on his back foot and leg. He felt better standing that way.

King threw. "Ball high," the coach called. "Full count."

"Put him away; nothing but K," the third baseman chattered.

Waiting in the box, rocking slightly on his back foot, Billy felt a slow-motion sensation come over him. On the last pitch he saw the ball all the way. He saw it leave King's hand. He saw it spinning. He saw its seams turning. He felt the way he did when he hunted ruffed grouse in the fall, with his small shotgun, walking along the leafy trail in October, knowing where the grouse would be. He knew when they would explode from the brush in a rush of wings.

Swinging the gun loose and balanced in his hand, he sometimes saw the grouse all the way: every brown-and-white feather, the black beads of its eyes, even the tiny claws of its feet. When a grouse rocketed out there were at the most two seconds to find it, swing and pull the trigger. Batting needed the same timing. And right now Billy's stick was cocked and ready to fire.

King Kenwood came down high and straight off the mound. Billy drove forward low and hard with his rear leg. His eyes followed the ball all the way to his bat. The ball floated in as large as a softball. For an instant he saw it bulge and flatten against the thick part of the bat—then it was gone with a hard, stinging *crack!*

King dove for cover. The ball whistled past his ear. Sprawled in front of the pitcher's mound, King watched Billy's ball rise straight out over second base toward center field.

The center fielder took one step back, then stopped. Hands hanging straight down at his sides, his mouth open, he turned to watch the ball soar overhead.

Billy stood at home plate, the bat still in his hand. The ball shrank away white against the gray-and-white clouds and disappeared far over the center-field fence.

"Holy cow!" the coach murmured. There was cheering from Billy's dugout.

The ball hit the tree in the front of the school, bounced high, disappeared atop the flat roof.

"That one's gone—for good!" the coach said.

Billy turned quickly to Coach Anderson. "I'm real sorry," he said. "I can pay for it."

The coach stared for a moment, then began to laugh. He kept laughing, doubling over, holding his knees.

"I can," Billy said stubbornly.

Coach Anderson pointed toward first base, wheezing. "Run, Baggs," he managed to say, "or you're out."

Billy dropped his bat and trotted, head down, around the bases.

At home plate, however, his teammates, with Tiny Tim at the front, were waiting for him. Blushing, Billy slapped their hands. He had no words, but the feeling of trotting around the bases felt natural. Like he had done it before. It gave him goose bumps. He thought of Robert. If only Robert had been here to see it.

His teammates cheered, and someone even honked a horn.

And kept honking.

The coach trotted over. "Billy that's for you, I think."

Billy looked up. Along the street, loaded and ready to head home, was the Baggses' truck and wagon. Their dusty old Ford truck and battered wagon piled high with bags of cattle feed. His father with his old greasy cap pulled low on his forehead. His mother there, too.

His father spit long and brown out the window. "Come on, boy—we got to git on home."

The other players stared.

Burning with embarrassment, Billy found his mitt. "Gotta go," he muttered, and walked away.

"I could come to your place!" Tiny Tim called after him.

The coach caught up with Billy at the truck.

"So how'd he do?" Abner said to Coach Anderson.

"One hit," the coach said. He smiled at Billy, who looked down at the ground.

"One hit. That's all?"

"He was only up to bat once," the coach replied. "A baseball game takes some time."

Abner looked at the sky, where the clouds had lightened. "Farm kids don't have all day," he said. "Plenty of work waitin' at home."

The coach thought a moment. "I've got an idea," he said. "I usually drop off a couple of boys after practice. Maybe I could drive Billy home."

"Nope," Abner said. "It's twenty miles, and we ain't in the habit of takin' free rides." He jerked his head at Billy. "You had your play time; now get in."

"Next Saturday?" the coach asked. "Will you folks be in town next Saturday? It's the last game of the season. Be nice to get Billy in for an inning or so."

"We might be comin' in. And we might not," Abner said.

The coach stared as Abner drove off. Billy sneaked a look in the rearview mirror. The coach stood there a moment, frowning. Then he turned, as he had to, back to the field. To the other boys.

CHAPTER NINE

As the Baggs family turned up their long driveway, Abner suddenly leaned forward over the steering wheel. He squinted ahead. "Damn!"

Billy looked. In the green, uncut alfalfa hayfield were three black-and-white Holstein heifers. Two of them raced about, stopping to gobble up mouthfuls of the thick alfalfa. One heifer lay on her side. Her white belly was puffed up. At the cow lot fence were the rest of the heifers. Skinnier heifers. They pressed against the fence Billy had fixed. The wires on one post looked wrong.

"Quick, get out and chase 'em back in!" Abner called to Billy and Mavis. "That fresh alfalfa will kill them."

Billy and his mother scrambled out of the pickup and into the field. They both knew that Abner was not exaggerating. Hay for cows should be dried, or cured, and then fed in bales. Or, if cows were pastured, there should be only lighter quack grass or Bromes grass for them to eat. Green alfalfa was too rich for their stomachs and caused gas, so much gas that they could bloat up and die within an hour.

The two heifers kept eating the fresh alfalfa as Billy and his mother ran toward them. At the last moment they leaped away, then snatched up more mouthfuls. The third heifer did not get up. Her belly was rounded up like she was pregnant. She let out a small, wheezing groan.

"I'll take care of her," Abner called angrily to Billy. "Just get those other two back in the lot."

Mavis ran to the gate and shooed the others to the rear of the lot. Skinner barked and nipped at the cattle as Billy chased the two heifers in wide circles. Finally they went back in. His mother locked the gate.

"Get me a darning needle—the longest one you got!" Abner shouted to Mavis. She hurried toward the house. Abner knelt over the heifer.

"And some matches," he called to Billy. Billy raced to the garage.

Back in a flash, panting, Billy handed the matches to Abner. The heifer's eyes were bugged out by now. She was panting harder than Billy, like her lungs were squeezed almost shut.

"Hurry up," Abner said to Billy's mother, who was nearing them.

"Light a match," Abner said to Billy.

Billy lit one and cupped his hands to steady its flame.

"Needle," Abner said to Mavis. She held out a long, silvery darning needle. "Hold it in the flame," Abner instructed.

While the needle heated, Abner ran his hand

slowly over the heifer's belly. He was counting ribs. "There," he murmured. Then he took up the needle and placed its point between two of the raised, lowest rib bones. With a quick punching motion he drove the needle through the skin and into the stomach.

A whistle of air came out. Hot, stinky, stomach gas spewed upward alongside the needle. Billy covered his nose. Abner worked the needle from side to side to keep the hole open. More gas hissed out. The heifer's belly deflated, but not all the way. The needle had gone into only one of its four stomach chambers.

"That's most of it," Abner muttered. "Maybe it's enough."

"Will she be all right?" Mavis asked.

"Jury's still out," Abner said. He looked back at the cow lot. "What about those other two?"

"They look okay," Billy said.

"We'll see," Abner said. He squinted at the wires Billy had fixed, at the wide gap near a middle post. "I thought you fixed that fence."

"I did."

"It don't look fixed to me," Abner growled.

Billy was silent.

"Get a halter rope," Abner said.

Billy got the rope and put it over the heifer's head and around her muzzle. They waited until the heifer tried to stumble to her feet. Then they pulled on the halter rope to help her get up. Billy and Mavis led her toward the barn.

"Put her in that far pen," Abner called after them. "We'll have to keep an eye on her." He turned away and limped back toward the pickup.

"I'm sorry," Billy's mother whispered. "This happenin' right after your ball game and all."

Billy shrugged.

"But she'll probably be okay," his mother added, touching her finger to the heifer's flank. There was a small blood spot where the needle had gone in.

"Maybe," Billy said. He smiled briefly as she ruffled his hair.

"Was baseball fun?" she asked softly, leaning closer.

He grinned from ear to ear, and nodded.

"Why am I whisperin'?" his mother said suddenly, and not to Billy. Mavis straightened up and looked back toward Abner and the truck. "Why do I always whisper?" she asked, louder this time.

After they had secured the heifer in the pen, Billy stepped outside the barn. Abner stood by the loosened wires of the fence, waiting.

Billy swallowed, and walked closer.

"You call this fence fixed?" Abner said.

Billy looked at the post.

Abner moved the two middle wires up and down easily with one hand.

There were no staples in them. Billy had forgotten to nail the middle wires on one of the posts. And the cattle, as cattle always did, had found the weak spot.

"Goes to show what happens when you got other things on your mind," Abner said harshly. "Like baseball and them Erickson girls."

Billy was silent.

"And if we hadn't a come home today when we did, all three of them heifers might be dead," Abner said. "All from you wantin' to goof around playin' baseball in town."

"You can't blame him," Billy's mother said, coming up behind him. She put her hands on Billy's shoulders.

"Who else is at fault, then?" Abner said.

"Maybe nobody. Maybe things just happen!" Her voice was loud and sharp, and she squeezed Billy's shoulders tighter and tighter as she talked. "And another thing. You run this place like it's some kind of army. Like Billy and me are . . . privates. Privates for life. Always on work detail."

As she spoke she shook Billy's shoulders, and his head jerked back and forth, like he was nodding in agreement. Abner glared down at him.

"Well you might be the general around here," Mavis said, "but I'm the—the—subgeneral. And it's time to get on with some things," she finished.

Abner straightened his neck as if to speak. But Mavis continued.

"This is 1970. Not 1950. And this family has got to start movin' ahead in the world. We been stalled ever since . . ." Her voice broke. "The rest of the world is movin' ahead and we're not," she said, recovering herself. "We're stalled along the road and the world is passin' us by. We're goin' thirty miles an hour and the world is goin' sixty."

Abner stared.

"That's because there's too much livin' in the past," Mavis said. "Too much lookin' in the rearview mirror."

They were all silent. Abner looked away.

Mavis spoke more softly now. "There's gotta be some changes around here," she said evenly. "There's gotta be and there's goin' to be."

Billy got the feeling she had been meaning to say these things for a long time. They had built up like water behind a beaver dam. Now, after one rain too many, the whole dam had burst.

Mavis looked about her now like she didn't know what to do. Then she turned on her heel and walked fast across the yard to the house. She did not look back.

Abner stared after her for a long time.

Billy was quiet as a field mouse.

Then Abner blinked. He turned and squinted down at Billy. "What's she mean, 'changes around here'?"

"I don't know," Billy said quickly.

Abner's eyes bored into Billy's.

"Honest!" Billy said.

Abner stared for a moment longer, then looked back at the house. "When it rains, it pours," he muttered. "Take another look at that heifer," he said to Billy, "and I'll go and see to your ma."

Billy watched as Abner limped toward the house. Then, first things first, he found a hammer and several wire staples. In a couple of minutes he had fixed the fence—for good this time. After he put away his tools he went back into the dim barn.

The barn was quiet.

Too quiet.

The heifer lay stretched out in the pen. At first Billy thought she was sleeping. Sleeping off her holiday in the alfalfa.

But by her nose was a wide spill of blood, like a red rug thrown on the straw. Pink bubbles covered her nose. They popped weakly as they died away. No new bubbles rose.

CHAPTER TEN

"I must have hit a vein with the needle." Abner said. He knelt on the crimson straw beside the dead heifer. "That's lung blood." He swore softly but not long.

Billy was silent. He stayed at arm's length from Abner, ready to run. Mavis stood a few steps farther back.

"So that's that, I guess," Abner said, staring down at the still animal. He was not angry, but calm, as if this bad luck was something expected. Like bad luck belonged to the Baggs farm. Like bad luck was the only thing in life their family could depend on.

"Help me roll her," Abner said to Billy.

Billy took a leg and rolled the heifer closer to the gate.

"Now bring the tractor around. We'll put her in the loader and take her out back. No use gettin' any more blood around here. Draws flies and makes the pigs crazy."

Billy hurried outside and climbed onto the little H Farmall tractor. He pulled out the ignition switch and the ring for the choke, pressed the starter button with his foot. Robert. He always felt Robert with him on the tractor. Robert had taught him to drive. Robert had . . . The engine coughed alive, and Billy worked the choke and stopped thinking. When the engine rpms were steady, he pulled back on the loader's lever. Big iron arms, one along each side of the tractor's nose, began to lift the front-end scoop. When the big scoop was raised a few inches off the ground, Billy pushed in the clutch pedal, put the H in first gear and drove the tractor carefully through the open barn door. He was a good driver. Really he was.

"Let down the bucket," Abner called.

Billy obliged. When the scoop scraped on concrete and straw, he set the brake and hopped down. Then he and Abner slid the heifer into the big bucket. Abner set a couple of skinning knives alongside the heifer. Then he pulled himself aboard, raised up the loader, and slowly backed the tractor from the barn.

Outside, Billy rode on the rear drawbar of the tractor; he stood upright, holding on to the iron seat where Abner swayed along. His father did not drive fast, and kept glancing down at Billy even though they weren't pulling anything behind them.

"I'm hangin' on," Billy said.

His father nodded and turned his face mostly forward again. The sun was shining. There was a nice breeze in their faces. Close alongside him, Billy could smell his father's body. A woody smell, like oak bark. It was not a bad smell. Every person had a scent, and oak bark was Abner's. They jolted along, the heifer's tail drooping from the bucket like a white rope, swaying with every bump. Out of sight of the house, Abner let the tractor roll to a stop.

On the ground they knelt over the heifer. Billy held the hind legs wide apart. Abner made a long slit up the belly. Then he reached in with both arms to cut away the heart and lung. His arms came back out shiny red. Billy pulled up handfuls of fresh grass and was ready with them. Abner took them to wipe his hands.

Billy helped cut away the gut sack from the pink stomach wall. The ribs shone pink and gray. When the gut sack was free, they hoisted the heifer by her front legs. The white guts and then the blood tumbled out and lay jiggling in the sunlight. The blood had already begun to thicken. It looked like dark cherry Jell-O. Flies dove toward the steaming pile.

"Save that liver," Abner said.

Billy stepped over to some brush and cut a thin forked branch with his knife. He peeled off its bark. Then he leaned down and fished out the liver. He cut it free from the intestines, then slid it over onto the clean grass, where he made a small slit through its biggest shiny gray lobe. Through the slit he poked one side of the forked branch. It made a perfect carrying stick.

Abner watched, wiping his forearms with more of the grass. "Not a lot of boys know how to fork a liver," Abner said. His teeth were brown from chewing tobacco. He was smiling.

When bad things happened, like this dead heifer, or a tractor breakdown, or a lightning-struck hog pen, that was when Billy felt closest to his father. Maybe it was because his father really needed his help then. Could not get by without him.

"We gonna skin her, too?" Billy said.

"You bet," Abner said, picking up his knife again. "No use wastin' her. She'll make some mighty good hamburger."

And so, with the heifer hanging upside down from the loader, they cut and peeled and rolled down the hide. The two of them worked easily on opposite sides of the heifer. Their knives circled close around each other but never touched. Their hands became slippery with tallow. The heavy hide began to droop on their arms. In ten minutes they trimmed around the neck. Finally their knives touched with a *click* and the hide fell away free.

Abner turned it hair side out and laid it on the grass. "We'll get three dollars for this hide. A pair of boots costs fifty. Figure that one out."

Billy helped him roll up the hide. Then they loaded the shining heifer back into the scoop.

Back in the farmyard, Abner carefully lowered the heifer onto a sheet of plastic Mavis had laid in the pickup's bed. The carcass slid out with a *dooomp!* Then Mavis smoothed a piece of cheesecloth over the fatty sides of the heifer to keep off the flies and dust. Billy handed her the liver.

"Too bad," she murmured.

"One of them things," Abner said pleasantly. "Me

and Billy will run her down to the locker plant."

Billy settled into the rider's side of the truck, and there was his baseball mitt. He quickly slid it out of sight beneath the seat; he did not want it to be connected with the bad luck.

As they rode along, he thought about the day. It did not seem like he had played baseball in town this morning. Billy wondered if he had only dreamed it. Hitting the home run. Watching the ball fly from his bat.

"Fresh liver and onions for supper tonight," Abner said as the pickup rattled along.

Billy smiled. He looked across the spring fields. At the buildings. The farm was bigger than any game. Its fields were bigger than any ball field. A dead heifer, the skinning and butchering, going to the locker plant—all of that was way bigger than a home run.

"Robert, he liked liver and onions," Abner said.

Billy said nothing. He did not look at his father.

"He could eat a whole fryin' pan of liver and onions," Abner said softly.

Billy continued to stare though the windshield. After a while Abner looked over at him. Billy felt his father's eye on him for long moments.

"It weren't your fault."

Billy stared down the road.

"You were small. No one blames you."

Billy was silent.

Abner turned off the corner, took the gravel road. They drove on in silence for at least a mile. Then Abner said, "This fall maybe we ought to go someplace. Drive out west. See the Black Hills."

Billy glanced at his father.

"They got buffalo in South Dakota, you know," Abner said.

Billy nodded.

"Balls on 'em big as church bells, they say."

Billy grinned a little.

Abner tried to laugh, but it came out in a short croak, almost like a sob. It was then Billy saw the deep water glistening in his father's eyes. When it trickled down Abner's cheeks, Billy looked away. He looked down and his own eyes burned.

"Maybe we should have done that long ago," Abner said hoarsely. "Right after it happened. Go someplace. Anyplace. Just get on the road and drive."

CHAPTER ELEVEN

Otto Howenstein, the butcher, was a stubby man with red hamburger under his fingernails. At sight of the heifer he shook his head and muttered "Scheisse" in German. He was never happy to see anyone, but he was a good butcher. His son, Shawn, who was Billy's age, stood stuffing sausage into long, clear guts; he and Billy jerked their heads at each other.

Otto opened the rear doors to the locker plant, and fog belled out. Otto rolled out the overhead carriage, ran two stainless-steel hooks through the heifer's hind legs, then hoisted her by a chain and pulley. The pulley made a ratcheting sound. Otto sent the heifer sailing into the cooler. In the fog hung other carcasses: two more cattle and three round white hogs.

"I'll be now working to midnight," Otto muttered.

"I appreciate you gettin' her in," Abner said.

Otto muttered something else.

Abner winked, and whispered to Billy, "He's sure a crabby old Kraut."

Billy smiled a little.

"Then again, who'd want to be a butcher?" Abner added.

Billy looked around. At the bones. At the blood.

On the way home Abner said, "That boy Shawn, you should invite him over sometime."

When they returned from the locker plant, there was no smell of liver and onions in the kitchen. There were sandwiches on the table and no plate at Mavis's place. Billy heard her typewriter clattering away. She was typing faster today than he had ever heard her. The noise sounded like the little lifters rattling inside a tractor's engine. Billy peeked into her sewing room.

"Everything go all right with Otto?" Mavis said, hardly moving her head as she typed.

"Just barely," Billy said.

"That's Otto," she said.

She kept typing.

"Supper is on the table," she added. She stared straight ahead at the wall and typed on. For several months the sewing machine had been stashed in the far corner. As she typed, she glanced down at the pages of a book that had writing like none Billy had ever seen. *Steno Exercises for Intermediates* it said at the top. Mavis squinted briefly at the strange writing, then looked back up at the wall. Her typing never stopped. "You have to see the whole paragraph at once," she explained to Billy, "and you can't look at the keys. It slows you down."

Billy nodded. Her keys kept *ratta-tat-tatt*ing, like a machine gun shooting out letters. "Supper is on the table," she repeated, louder this time.

Billy backed out of the room. In the kitchen, Abner stood outside the sewing-room door, listening.

"What's she typin' this time?" he asked. He kept his voice low.

Billy shrugged. "Steno."

Abner shook his head. "Last winter it was the Sears catalogue," he muttered. "This spring the telephone book. Pages and pages of telephone numbers. Now this stuff—what do you call it?"

"Steno. Stenography."

"Ste-no-gra-phy," Abner repeated.

"It looks like Russian or something," Billy said.

"Or Chinese," Abner said, shaking his head discouragedly. He headed toward the dinner table. "Your ma's gone around the bend. Maybe she ought to see one of them whatayacallems—headshrinks."

"Psychiatrists," Billy said, thinking of Tiny Tim.

"Them," Abner said.

They sat down at the table. Abner did not take off his cap, something Mavis never let him get away with. He let out a long breath, then bowed his head. "Lord, deliver us of your infernal invention, the typewriter. Amen."

Abner never said grace. That was Mavis's job. Billy began to giggle. Abner had the beginnings of a grin himself.

The typewriter keys went quiet. "I heard that!" came Mavis's voice.

Abner looked up, looking guilty.

She appeared in the doorway. "First, take off your cap."

Abner did.

"Second, you'd better not be takin' the Lord's name in vain. We don't make a real big deal of Him around here, but you never know, do you?"

Abner glanced sideways at Billy.

"Third, you won't be makin' fun of me when I start bringin' home a paycheck," she said.

"Paycheck?" Abner said.

"Paycheck?" Billy echoed.

"Paycheck," Mavis said. She stood with her hands on her hips.

Billy and Abner looked at each other.

"You're always complainin' about making ends meet around here. Billy's near grown-up nowadays. So this morning I interviewed for a job. In town."

"A job?" Abner said.

"In town?" Billy added quickly.

"That's right, in town," Mavis said, stepping forward and beginning to pass around more cold cuts. Then she stopped as if she had remembered something. She pushed the meat and cheese and mayo forward so they could make up their own sandwiches.

"What job? Where?" Billy asked.

"At Doctors' Clinic. A while back there was an ad in the paper for a secretary."

Abner's lips moved several times before any words

came out. "You ain't never been a secretary."

"That's true," Mavis said.

"You don't know anything about being a secretary," Abner said, louder this time.

"I been typin' every night for a year."

Billy glanced sideways at Abner.

"Seventy words a minute with one error," she said proudly. "And I can take shorthand dictation, too."

"Steno," Abner said.

Mavis nodded.

Abner glanced at Billy. He sat up straighter in his chair now. Suddenly he looked down at the cold cuts. At the sack of bread, the jar of mayo. "Is this how we're supposed to eat around here while you're . . . in town?"

"Like I said, there will have to be some changes," Mavis said.

Abner raised an eyebrow.

"But don't worry; nobody's goin' to starve to death," Mavis said. "I got it pretty much all figured out."

"How so?" Abner asked immediately.

"No use to worry about a thing until it happens," Mavis said. "That's what you always say, I believe, isn't it?"

Abner harrumphed and pointed to the cold cuts. "Better eat up, Son; it might be slim pickin's around here."

"I don't even know if I'll get the job," Mavis said. She turned away, looked out the window.

Abner perked up some. He looked briefly at Billy.

"Just an interview, then," he said, spearing a slice of cheese.

"That's all," she said.

"Maybe nothin' will come of it," Abner said. He pointed to the loaf of bread, the bologna. Billy passed it.

"Maybe not," she said. Mavis turned again to face them. "But maybe."

Abner stared. "When will you know?"

"Monday."

Billy thought. Today was still Saturday. Then there was Sunday. It was going to be a long weekend. He would make sure to be out of the house as much as possible.

"Monday," Abner muttered to himself, finally taking a bite of a giant sandwich. He said it like Monday was Doomsday.

The rest of Saturday passed quickly enough. Abner and Billy had hay to bale.

Billy rode the wagon. Ahead came the baler. Ahead of the baler was the big tractor, which Abner drove. The tractor powered the baler and pulled everything along. Billy rode on the swaying wagon, his feet set wide apart for balance. He waited for the bales and thought about his mother.

Her town job.

Her "maybe" town job.

If she got the job in town, how would she get there? They had only one vehicle, the farm pickup.

He looked up at Abner, who rode along sideways on the tractor's seat, watching the baler, looking first ahead and then behind. Sometimes Abner forgot and stared off across the field. Or scowled back toward the house. The baler veered wide to the right and almost missed the hay windrow. Billy decided he would not ask any questions.

He rode along and caught the bales one by one. They moved toward him in short, jerky steps. Up the baler's chute to its shiny end—then a tip down onto the smooth wooden boards of the wagon. There Billy grabbed the twines and bucked each bale backward. He chose a spot for each bale as he went. Every bale weighed about fifty pounds, and the stubble prickled his forearms, but he didn't think about that, either. Baling was routine. A rhythm. The tractor's engine hummed. The baler's pickup teeth clattered in a never-ending, backward circle that lifted the green windrow from the ground. The intake auger *shush-shush*ed the hay into the long chamber. The square plunger fist punched forward and backward and forward with its own regular rhythm. And every couple of minutes there was the clatter and swinging of gears as the twine looped around the bale and knotted itself. In a slow, steady crawl, the hay flowed up through the baler onto the wagon. Riding the wagon during baling was not the worst job on the farm. Billy's hands knew what to do, which left his mind free to think.

And right now there was plenty to think about.

What would it be like to be alone with Abner all day? (How would they eat?)

Was there now more chance to play baseball, or less? (There had to be more chance, he decided. He could catch a ride to town with Mavis—and a ride home, too.)

In the middle of these thoughts his father shouted and braked the tractor. Billy stumbled forward, nearly falling off the deck of the wagon. From the baler's chute rose a twisted bale with only one twine.

"You're supposed to be watchin'!" Abner called.

Billy quickly hopped down and opened the twine box. He found a spare piece. Back at the bale chute, he reached underneath, felt along the warm, smooth metal. Found the broken string. Then he tied a slip knot and pulled the bale back into shape—not as tightly as the baler pressed them, but good enough. Last, he tied the strings.

"Keep your eyes peeled next time," Abner said as he put the tractor in gear once again.

Slowly, as they worked into the evening, the bales became heavier. It was a gradual change, like the tide coming in or the sun setting. And it was not because Billy's arms were tired now. Each bale now clearly weighed several more pounds than the others had an hour ago. He looked up the sky. It was cooler, with a slight dampness in the air. The hay was drawing moisture from the evening sky.

"How are they?" Abner called.

"A little heavy."

"Loosen her up two turns."

Billy hopped down and, trotting along the baler's chute, loosened its chamber. He did this by turning two handles that looked like sideways bicycle pedals. When loosened counterclockwise, they reduced hay compression in the chamber. This meant less hay per bale, and lighter bales. If hay was baled too tightly when it was damp, or even baled loosely when it was wet, the hay heated inside the bale. Heat meant mold. Too much heat meant the real possibility of fire. Spontaneous combustion, it was called. In a hayloft, one wagonload of damp, heavy bales pressed down deeply beneath two thousand more bales, could catch fire and burn down a barn.

So they went on, slower now, for one last round. The wagon was nearly full anyway, and the stacking was always difficult at the end. Billy struggled to heave the last bales high up on the wagon. Two bales backed up beside the chute and threatened to fall off. His father slowed the tractor slightly.

"Enough?" Abner called.

Billy shook his head stubbornly. He was big enough to load a full wagon by himself. With nobody's help, certainly not Abner's. He worked faster, now, panting.

Just before he lost the battle with the oncoming bales, his father swung away from the windrow and pulled the baler out of gear. "Gettin' too late," he called back to Billy. "Let's go home."

Billy sat down, sweating. On the way home he took his time stacking the last bales. He crisscrossed the bales so they would not fall off. He liked a perfectly square wagonful. He thought of the miller, his clever knot. The butcher with his smooth steel hook, and the way he swung the heifer into the foggy cooler. When Billy was finished stacking, he was all the way on top, six bales above the wagon floor. And there he rode home, the breeze cool on his damp forehead and his shirt. He was king, at least for a few minutes, of his own wagon.

At home Mavis came out to help unload. It was important to get the hay under cover in case of rain. Outside the barn, Abner pulled the hay wagon close alongside the elevator, a long, skinny conveyor that looked like an aluminum ladder leaning against the barn. A chain stretched along the middle. Large gears on either end of the conveyor, the bottom one connected to a small electric motor, turned the chain. The long chain had short prongs about every three feet. Three little fingers hooked into the hay bale and carried it upward through a small door into the hayloft.

"We can get 'em," Abner said shortly as Mavis approached. She wore her garden coveralls and carried her gloves.

"I'll help," she said. "I'll tumble them down to you."

"Wouldn't want to damage those million-dollar fingers of yours," Abner said.

"Maybe they are," Mavis said sharply.

"Humph," Abner muttered.

Billy watched.

"You'll see," she said, pulling on her gloves.

Abner spit and motioned to Billy. "Plug it in, else we'll be working in the dark."

"Which wouldn't be the first time," Mavis said.

Billy quickly joined the two ends of the cord, and

the chain jerked forward. Its clattering crawl began, and Billy hurried up to the hayloft.

Which was not his favorite place.

There the air was warm and stuffy. He set himself for the first bale, which already creaked along above him. It reached the end of the conveyor, teetered, then tipped forward. It fell with a thud and a puff of dust, and Billy trotted it backward to the far wall. Just as he returned, the next bale thudded down.

He trotted steadily back and forth with the bales. He heard his parents' voices coming from outside. For a while they were loud; then they didn't speak at all. Once, no bales came up the elevator; Billy went to the doorway for a peek down.

"Mrs. Pederson drives right by the farm every mornin' and night. She works in town." Mavis was saying.

"We don't need free rides from anybody."

"If I get the job, the bank will give me a loan for a used car."

"Banks—you think banks are there to help you? Banks are not nobody's friend."

"They helped me get the typewriter," she said.

"What!?" Abner said.

"I didn't tell you because you'da just said 'No,'" Mavis said. She tumbled down a bale. Abner had to hop aside.

"So we owe money at the bank?"

"No—I got it paid off already. With my egg money."

Abner muttered something, turned back to the conveyor. He began to throw bales on it, one after another. Billy ducked back into the hayloft and got ready.

Soon he wished his parents were talking again. When they did, there was time for him to get a breath between bales, but when they were silent the bales came up the elevator with hardly a space between them.

Billy began to dart back and forth. Dust increased in the tall arch of the barn. Sweat ran down his back, and he itched. His face was streaked with dust. Bales began to pile up below the tip of the elevator. At first two, then four, then five. Then a small mountain. As he raced back and forth, he became madder and madder at his parents.

Suddenly he stomped to the hayloft door. He took the electric cord in his hand and gave it a sharp jerk. The elevator stopped dead.

His parents looked up.

"Slow down, dammit!" he shouted at them. "I ain't Superman!"

They stared up at him. He swallowed. He realized he had just sworn at his parents. Now he was in deep trouble.

But his parents glanced briefly at each other. Then Abner straightened to his full height.

Billy thought the hayloft might not be so bad a place after all. He might have to hide out there tonight.

"I guess," Abner said, "we . . . we just kind of . . ."

"Forgot," Mavis murmured. "About you. Sorry."

Billy shrugged. "It's okay," he said. "It's okay. Just give me a few minutes to catch up."

"Take your time," Abner said.

As Billy turned back to the hayloft, he saw Abner and Mavis sit down on the bales and look at each other.

CHAPTER TWELVE

Sunday passed as slowly as winter honey dripping off a spoon. Sunday was Abner's and Billy's least favorite day. Though the Baggs family did not belong to any church, Mavis would not let them work on Sunday. "Some parts of the Bible make sense," she said, "and other parts are plumb strange. But the part about restin' on the seventh day, now that one was made for country folks."

On Sunday mornings, after milking and breakfast, Abner sat in the middle of the kitchen or else paced around in the house. He went to the stove for another cup of coffee. He went to the window to check the weather. The brighter the sunshine outside, the blacker the cloud that seemed to hang over Abner's head. He sighed. He cleaned his nails with his jackknife, which made a loud scraping sound. Finally Mavis would send Abner out with some small chore, such as dumping potato peelings into the chicken pen. "And take your time about it," Mavis would add.

Getting the message, Abner usually hung out by

the corral fence, inspecting the young stock and having a chew of Copenhagen tobacco. Or else he drove in the pickup out along the fields, looking. Looking at the crops. Looking at the fence lines. Looking for fresh gopher mounds.

Billy had no such luck. He had to stay inside Sunday morning and wear his good school clothes. Every week Mavis assigned him a part of the Bible to read. Then on Sunday morning he and Mavis read it aloud together and discussed it. Today it was the book of Ruth.

"Now take Ruth," Mavis said. "Sometimes I think there was somethin' wrong with that woman. Whyever would she . . ."

Billy got into the habit of asking his mother questions. This usually started her talking and so let him off the hook. Whenever his mother got up to baste the chicken that was roasting, or start a flame beneath the potato pan, Billy yawned behind his hand and leaned sideways to check the weather outside.

"All that Ruth did was work, work, work," Mavis said from the stove. "No wonder she ran off and left her family and they starved to death."

"They did?" Billy said, suddenly sitting up straighter.

Mavis raised one eyebrow at him.

Billy grinned sheepishly and bent closer over the pages. There really were some pretty good stories in the Bible. When he was younger, he always asked his mother the same question: Were the stories true?

And Mavis's answer was always the same. "Maybe they were, maybe they weren't."

At noon there was the usual large meal. Roasted chicken. Riced potatoes. Billy's job was to squeeze the boiled potatoes through the ricer. He liked to watch the little white potato worms squirt into the bowl. And there were pickles, dill and beet. Buns, homemade of course. Gravy in the white gravy boat, Jell-O, and blueberry pie.

After dinner Billy helped his mother do dishes. Abner sat cleaning his teeth with a toothpick. When the dishes were done, his parents usually went to their bedroom for a nap.

This Sunday afternoon Abner sawed logs on the couch. Mavis went into the bedroom. Billy knew they were still arguing over Mavis's town job. And Billy was left with nothing to do, as usual.

He looked for a while at the Sears catalogue, spending some time in the women's pages. Then he looked at the sports equipment in the back. He looked at gloves. At bats.

Soon he went outside. In the quiet, sunbaked yard, Skinner dozed in the shade of his little slab house. Even the barn swallows were resting. They sat on the fence in a row like clothespins on a line.

Skinner groaned and rolled over in the dirt. He was old now, and had hardly any teeth left. Too much chewing on beaver skeletons and other farm bones.

Somewhere a cicada buzzed, the first one of the summer.

Billy sat on the front step and whittled on a stick with his jackknife. Starting with no aim, gradually he found himself carving something. A stick thick at one end. Thin on the other. With a small knob at the very end of the handle. A bat.

He looked up, across the yard, at his father's sawmill. "Skinner—come on!" he called.

Skinner scrambled up from the dirt, expecting a rabbit or a stray calf. Seeing nothing, he still trotted after Billy to the sawmill.

"Good dog, Skinner."

Among the lumber piles Billy began to search for the right piece. A real bat probably should be ash, he knew, but he would start with pine. Soft yellow pine that he could carve easily. He passed up and down the piles, hefted this timber and that, then spotted it: a straight-grained, blocky piece of pine four feet long and four inches square.

First with a hatchet, then with a drawknife, he worked on the wood. Yellow shavings fell onto his shoes—his Sunday shoes—and he got sap on his pants. He worked on, squeezing the bat between his legs, pulling the broad knife along its shaft. Skinner snored beside Billy's feet. Occasionally he trembled and huffed his floppy lips in a dream. "Rabbits," Billy murmured, without looking away from his work. "Get them rabbits."

"What are you makin'?" a teasing voice said. "Looks weird to me."

Skinner woofed and Billy jerked around. He almost cut his hand.

Gina Erickson stood a few steps behind him.

Billy looked back at the bat, which stuck up from

his lap. "Real funny, twerp. It's a baseball bat."

"Looks like somethin' else to me," Gina said, and giggled.

"You know, you got the dirtiest mind of any eleven-year-old kid I know," Billy said. He took the half-carved bat from his lap.

"Almost twelve," she said.

"So you're still young enough for a spanking," Billy said, pointing the stick at her, "which is what you're gonna get if you keep sneakin' up on me."

"You wouldn't dare."

Billy dove sideways.

Gina shrieked as Billy caught her ankle. She fell, laughing, in the soft sawdust.

"I wouldn't dare, huh?" Billy said, staring down at her.

"If you wanna spank me, you got to pull down my pants," Gina said.

"Geez!" said Billy, disgusted. He let her go, got up and brushed off his knees. "Like I said, your mind—"

"I'm just advanced for my age," Gina said, resting on her elbows. She glanced down at her T-shirt, moved her eyes from side to side. "All over."

"Is that all you think about?" Billy said.

"What?"

"It," Billy said.

"It's all anybody thinks about when they're big," Gina said. "Your folks are probably in their bedroom right now, doin' it."

"Why, you little—" Billy said angrily. He grabbed for her again but she darted away, behind a pile of boards. The boards were stacked crisscross for drying. Billy could see her between the layers as they circled the pile. Billy went one way, then another, but she was too fast for him.

"Okay, I give up," Billy said. He pretended to lose interest.

"Boys never give up," Gina said, staying just out of reach.

Billy smiled to himself. She was not dumb, this little twerp.

"Anyway, I'm goin' swimmin' at Riverbend. Heather is there right now," Gina said.

"So?" Billy said, turning back to his bat, his shavings.

"So she didn't take along her swimsuit."

Billy glanced back at Gina. He shrugged. "I might come. But right now I'm workin'."

"On your big bat?"

"Beat it!" Billy said. He grabbed a shovel and heaved a large scoop of sawdust over the pile. Gina hollered and scampered farther off.

"I'll tell her you like bats better than real girls."

"Don't you tell her anything!" Billy threatened.

Gina grinned and stuck out her tongue.

Billy began to race after her, but she jumped on her bike and soon outdistanced him. He stopped and watched her red head shrink away down the road toward the trees and the river.

He worked another few minutes, looking occasionally across the field to the trees where Gina had disappeared. He wondered if she was lying. Probably.

He gave his new bat several more strokes with the drawknife. Then suddenly he stood up and brushed away the shavings. "Come on, boy," he said.

Skinner and Billy approached Riverbend. There was a narrow path that led through the trees. He wished he had left Skinner home. "Heel!" he whispered. Skinner looked up, confused. Billy had no partridge gun, but Skinner heeled anyway.

Billy walked along slowly now. He tried to see through the leaves to the river. He crouched lower as they neared the blue sparkle of water. The big rocks where farm kids swam, and where Heather ought to be, were empty.

"Looking for someone?!" voices shouted from above them. Mud showered down, splattering on Billy's head and on Skinner's back.

They yelped and leaped ahead, into the open, away from the ambush. Gina and Heather's laughter came down from the branches of the tree. He saw their bare white feet standing on a limb.

"I hope you scratch your asses good on the way down," Billy called.

The girls laughed harder.

Billy spit out mud. He had mud in his hair, on his shoulders and down his back. On the river's rocks he knelt down and took off his shirt. As he rinsed off, behind him he heard a branch snap and a sudden shriek.

There was swearing, then silence. He kept rinsing his shirt.

"Billy," Gina called, "Heather can't get down."

"Sure," Billy said.

"No, really."

"She got up there, she can get herself down."

"Come on, Billy."

"You ambush me and I'm supposed to help her down?"

"Just stand so she can step on your shoulders."

Billy took his time dipping his head in the water, rinsing his hair. When he looked back, he saw Gina swing down and drop several feet to the ground. She waited, staring up into the tree. She looked over at Billy.

"All right," Billy said. He walked over and looked up into the tree.

Heather Erickson was wearing her white two-piece bathing suit. The bottoms of her feet were dirty. Her strong, stubby legs were scratched by tree branches. Over the skimpy top of her bathing suit she stared down. Her eyes were wide and round and framed by her red hair.

"Sit down on the branch and it won't seem so far down," Gina said.

"Shut up," Heather said.

"Listen to your sister," Billy said.

"You shut up too, Billy Baggs. Just get me down from here," Heather said.

"I might help you down, but how do I know you're Heather?" Billy said.

"What!" Heather said. "Who else would I be?"

"Gina said you weren't wearing a swimsuit."

"Well, I am," Heather snapped.

"But maybe you're somebody else," Billy said.

Gina giggled.

There was silence, then a rustling among the branches. A white bathing suit top fluttered down.

"There," Heather said.

Billy stepped forward quickly, ready to help.

"Make her go all the way!" Gina whispered loudly to Billy.

"You're dead meat," Heather shouted at her sister.

Billy paused briefly, then reached up his hands. "Step on my hands, then drop."

"I'm scared."

"I'll catch you."

Heather took a breath. Shrieking, she dropped, and Billy caught her. She was soft and bouncing and white and she smelled like river water.

"Let go of me!" Heather shouted. She cuffed Billy alongside the head.

"You're the one who wanted help," Billy said, ducking away.

Heather snatched up her top and held it up to herself. "Where is that little shit?" she asked, looking around.

"Nanna nanna na na," came Gina's voice from the brush.

Billy laughed.

"She drives me crazy."

"Me, too," Billy said.

Heather stared at him as she fit herself into the two white cups. "Sorry about the mud pies."

Billy grinned. "Good ambush. I was dead."

"Maybe you had your mind on something else."

Billy shrugged. He blushed.

Heather giggled, with the same kind of laugh as Gina's. She turned her back to Billy and held out the strings. "Tie me."

Billy stepped forward and tied the little strings. His hands shook slightly, but he managed to finish the knot.

"Anyway, you still got to see what you came for," Heather said, turning back to Billy.

Billy was silent. He knew his neck and cheeks were as red as her hair.

"So?"

"So what?" Billy said.

"What do you think?" Heather said. She glanced down at herself.

Billy swallowed again. "You're beautiful," he said. His eyes widened. He hadn't meant to say that.

"I can see you mean that," Heather said sarcastically, staring down at Billy's pants.

He blushed deeper and bent forward to minimize the problem.

"You thirteen-year-olds," Heather said, clucking her tongue. "You're so . . . desperate." She turned and headed toward the river. "Now beat it, Billy Baggs, so I can have some privacy."

Billy stood there. Skinner cocked his head at him. "Come on, boy," Billy finally said. He and Skinner left the river behind and headed back across the open fields. But Billy kept looking back to the trees. To the river. The weather felt hotter than ever.

CHAPTER THIRTEEN

Monday morning, Abner worked in the second hayfield. The tractor engine hummed. The mower kept up its steady *chakachakachaka* sound. Hay fell over the sickle in a continuous green wave.

Billy sat impatiently in the rear of the truck and filed the second sickle with short, jerky strokes. Skinner snoozed beside Billy's feet; suddenly he woofed and looked up. Billy raised his head.

Mavis. She was running full speed toward them. Down the lane and up to them. Long strides. Billy stood up. He had never seen her run before. Her chest bounced and her feet ate up the ground. She could really run!

"I got it!" she cried. "They called and I got the job." She bounded right into the back of the pickup and swept him off his feet. For what felt like ten minutes she jigged him around the truck. He felt her strong arms and soft front. He couldn't breathe.

"Good, Ma, good!" Billy said, trying to get free.

Down the field, Billy saw Abner's straight swath of hay begin to curve. Abner was looking back at them dancing in the pickup bed. Billy saw him swing the mower away from the hay and turn the tractor around. He was coming back.

Abner drew near on the tractor. Mavis swallowed and looked at Billy. Then she moved her feet wider apart, like she was riding a swaying wagon.

Close by, now, Abner reached down and shut off the engine switch. Except for the rasp of grasshoppers the field was silent.

"Looks like I got the job," Mavis said casually.

Abner was silent.

"So what do you think?" she said. There was an eagerness in her voice that she couldn't hold back.

Abner shrugged. "So what does it pay?"

"Three dollars an hour."

"Less tax," Abner said. He folded his arms across the steering wheel and stared.

Mavis shrugged.

"Less driving expense."

"With a raise after thirty days," Mavis said defensively.

"Less new clothes, probably," Abner continued.

Mavis was silent. She looked down briefly at her everyday dress.

"You'd be lucky to clear a dollar fifty an hour," Abner said, and spit. "You could make that much sellin' eggs."

"I hate selling eggs," Mavis said softly. "People come driving in here. Seeing me all the time in coveralls and work gloves. A fork or a shovel in my hand." Her voice got louder. "Don't you think I got pride?"

Abner sat up slightly on the tractor's seat.

"Don't you think I might want to wear a dress sometime for a whole day? And have hands that don't look rough as corncobs?"

Abner was silent. His eyes flickered briefly to Billy.

"I used to be *pretty*," she said, her voice breaking slightly. "You said so. At least you used to. That's part of why you married me."

Abner looked away.

"Then after—after Robert, I didn't care how I looked," Mavis said. "For quite a while nothing mattered."

"Billy," Abner said, "I need another tube of grease. Head on back to the shop."

"But now I do care," Mavis said. "I'm only thirty-five and I still care how I look."

"Billy!" Abner said.

"I'm goin', I'm goin'," Billy said. Walking away, he turned several times to look back. His parents kept talking at each other. His mother used her hands, her arms. Abner still held on to the steering wheel of the tractor. Once when Billy turned, he saw that Abner had lowered his head onto his hands. His father sat there, cradling the wheel, his head down, like he did not know in which direction to steer.

For a Monday, dinner was extra large. It was like a Sunday dinner. Hot roast beef, all the trimmings.

They ate, but no one said anything.

Finally Abner spoke. "So when would you start?"

"They'd like me to come in this afternoon, get the lay of things," Mavis said. "After that, right away."

"Right away," Abner said.

She swallowed. "Tomorrow."

Abner narrowed his eyes. He turned to Billy. Billy looked down at his plate and kept eating.

"What do you think?"

Billy looked up. "Me?"

Abner waited.

Billy tried to swallow his potatoes. His parents both looked at him. "I dunno. We can get along probably," he said. "I can cook potatoes."

Mavis smiled a tight smile.

"And roast beef? And pie?" Abner thundered.

Billy was silent.

"He don't have to be the cook," Mavis said. "I got that figured out."

"Well I'm glad we ain't gonna starve. That's some progress."

"So I need to drive in this afternoon." Mavis said, keeping the conversation going. "Then tomorrow I'll ride with Mrs. Pederson."

Abner looked up sharply.

"She and I already talked," Mavis said. "I'm paying her with eggs and garden vegetables."

Abner was silent.

"I'll ride with her for a while, see how that works out."

"And if it don't?" Abner said.

"We'll wait and see," Mavis said calmly. She lifted

a large slice of roast beef onto Abner's place, then pushed the gravy boat his way. "You'd better eat up," she said with a tiny wink to Billy. "No tellin' when we'll have roast beef again."

That afternoon Billy rode along with Mavis. She wore her blue-and-white dress. Her hair was pinned up in back and her perfume smelled like wild roses, the pale pink kind that grew along the roads. She carried her *Steno Exercises for Intermediates* book. "Just in case," she said to Billy.

Billy held up his baseball mitt. "Just in case," he said.

They laughed and drove away. At the highway Mavis paused to look both ways, then back toward the farm. The sun was shining; the skies were clear. "We're striking out, Billy. You and me, we're finally striking out on our own."

Billy smiled.

"Ready?" Mavis asked.

Billy laughed. "Let 'er rip."

Mavis did. She punched the gas pedal to the floor and dropped the clutch and the truck roared sharply forward. Its tires spun on gravel, then burned rubber as she turned onto the tar. Mavis laughed again, and drove seventy miles an hour all the way to town.

They parked by Doctors' Clinic, a low, red-brick building. Mavis made no move to get out. She stared through the windshield.

Billy waited.

"What am I doing?" she murmured to herself.

"You're goin' to work, Ma."

She turned suddenly, hugged Billy's head sharply to her breast, and got out. He smelled roses again. "Yes. I am. And you're goin' to play ball or do whatever you please for a change," she said. She opened her purse and gave Billy a whole dollar. "Things are changing, Billy," she said.

Billy watched her climb the short flight of steps and go inside the clinic. Then he tucked the dollar into his shoe and headed toward the baseball field.

CHAPTER FOURTEEN

Practice was well under way. Coach Anderson waved Billy onto the field. Tiny Tim Loren raced up like he was going to hug Billy or something similarly stupid. "Back off," Billy said, ready to stiff-arm the pest.

"Sure, Billy," Tiny Tim said with a grin. And he skipped along beside Billy as they crossed the grass.

"Rag Baggs is back," Nix Nixon called.

Billy set his jaw and walked on by.

"Back in right field," Tim shouted to Nix, "where you used to be."

Nixon stopped throwing and stared at Billy. "Let him try."

"Dry up, dammit," Billy muttered to Tim. "You want everybody to hate me or somethin'?"

"They do already," Tim said cheerfully, "'cause they know you're going to be better than them."

"Not if I get thrown off the team for smashin' in somebody's face," Billy said. "So pipe down."

"Sure, Billy," Tim said.

They passed by King Kenwood.

"Hey, King," Tim said. "When you pitch today, be sure to wear a batting helmet. Billy's here."

King Kenwood ignored him.

Tiny Tim skipped out of Billy's reach. "Anyway, I thought you said you couldn't come to town."

"You keep botherin' me, I won't."

"That means you can come over to my house," Tiny Tim said.

Billy stopped and stared down at this mosquito. Last time he was too nice to him. "Maybe I don't want to," Billy said. "Now get lost, you runt. Beat it!"

Tiny Tim kept smiling.

Coach Anderson trotted over. "Tim, take center field today."

"Center field? Far out—really far out—get it?" Tim laughed his shrill laugh.

"I get it, Tim," the coach said. "I get it."

As Tim raced off, the coach stared after him. Then he turned to Billy. "Tim has some problems. Some special needs. Maybe you noticed."

Billy was silent.

"About five years ago his parents were killed in a car crash."

Billy's eye widened.

"He was with them," the coach added. "A particularly bad accident. They had to cut him out, and there was fire, too. He saw everything."

Billy looked out toward Tiny Tim, who was

putting dandelions around his cap brim and calling to the left fielder to look.

"If he's too much bother, let me know," the coach said.

Still staring at Tim, Billy said, "He ain't that much bother."

The coach warmed up with Billy, and they talked. "So what brings you to town on a Monday?"

"My ma got a town job."

"Great," the coach said. "That means you can make regular practice."

"Most days," Billy said. "Except for baling."

The coach nodded. "We've got one game left, on Saturday. Then that's it for the season—unless we go to playoffs. So we better get you into the groove starting right now."

"What about the work?" Billy said.

"The work?" the coach said.

"The paintin'. The eighteen bucks I owe. I have to work it out."

"Oh, yes," the coach said. He nodded with an exaggerated motion. "I hadn't forgotten about the eighteen dollars."

"When do I start the paintin'?"

"Tomorrow," Coach Anderson said. "The paint . . . the paint didn't come in to the lumberyard yet. They expect it this afternoon. Besides," the coach said, looking up at the sky, testing the air with his hand, "it's a little humid today."

Billy glanced up at the sky. It was sunny and cloud-less.

"Right now we got baseball to think about," Coach Anderson said. He looked out at the infield, then back at Billy. "Have you ever played third base?"

After they warmed up, Billy adjusted his cap and crouched at third base. It was infield practice. The coach tossed up a ball, then *ding*ed it toward him. Billy snared the ball and threw it on the run—high over the first baseman's head.

There were whistles and a hoot or two.

"Wildman Baggs!"

"E-five!" several boys shouted. Billy did not know what that meant. What the numbers stood for. And he didn't ask.

The coach trotted out. "Make sure you set, plant yourself, then throw," he said. He demonstrated. "Set. Plant. Throw."

Billy nodded and got ready again.

Back at home plate, the coach chopped another grounder Billy's way.

Billy scooped the ball, braced and threw. It was a hard throw, belt high and fast. The first baseman, Jake Robertson, stretched straight ahead for it—then at the last moment raised his glove. The ball skipped off the top of his glove and bounced into right field.

"E-five!" Nix Nixon hooted. "Nice throw, Baggs!"

"More like E-three," the coach said. "Jake—stay

with it," he called to the first baseman.

Billy realized that each field position had a number.

Jake Robertson, a skinny left-hander who also pitched, held up his arms in protest. "The ball had *stuff*. It rose a foot," he said.

Coach Anderson turned his gaze back to Billy, who looked down and slapped his glove.

"So it ain't my error," Jake called, "not with stuff like that."

"Isn't," the coach murmured, as he looked at Billy.

"I probably ain't any good at third base," Billy said. "If I throw it too hard, the ball don't go straight."

"How so?" the coach asked.

"I dunno," Billy said. He just wanted to get on with things. Not be the center of attention. "It just don't."

"Doesn't," the coach said.

Billy stared.

"Baseball has rules; grammar has rules," the coach said. "Sometimes we work on both, all right? I'm a full-service kind of coach."

Billy blushed and nodded.

"Anyway, show me how it doesn't go straight," the coach said. He trotted over to first base and handed the bat to Jake. "Go hit a grounder to Billy."

"Sure," Jake said immediately. He glanced at King Kenwood.

"Burn it," King whispered as Jake trotted to home plate.

Jake winked at him. "Ready?" he called to Billy.

Billy nodded.

Jake slashed a grounder to Billy's right, in deep third. With a dive Billy managed to get a piece of the ball, but it spun away down the left-field line.

"E-five!" Nix shouted. King Kenwood smiled.

"This is practice, Jake," the coach said evenly. "A ground ball, not a base hit."

"Sorry," Jake said, with a guilty grin. He tossed up another ball. This one he hit hard and straight, a skipping grounder to Billy. Billy caught it cleanly. Planted. Leaned hard into his throw, a throw that rose a good six inches at the last moment and stung the palm of the coach's hand like a wet leather strap.

Coach Anderson caught the ball just off his belt. He stared across at Billy. In all his years in summer baseball he had never seen a ball hop like that.

He trotted back to home plate. "Nice throw, Baggs," he said casually. He tossed the ball to Jake. "See? Nothing to it. Just stay with it next time."

"Sure," Jake muttered. He looked out at Billy. "Stuff like that, he ought to be pitchin'."

There was silence.

King Kenwood stared at Jake without expression.

"Or center field or something," Jake added quickly.

"Play ball, boys," the coach called. He hit grounders around the infield and then flies to the outfield to finish practice. He kept hitting to everyone, but Billy got the idea that Coach Anderson was, for some reason, watching mostly him that afternoon.

———

Toward the end of practice, cars began to arrive as mothers came to get their boys. Shiny town cars. Even a convertible or two. The mothers wore shorts and bright summer tops and sunglasses. Their legs were very tanned. Their hair was short and puffed up fashionably high and round. They didn't look anything like Mavis. The moms looked more like the women in the catalogue.

But Billy would bet that Mavis was tougher than any of them. He thought of her bounding down the lane toward the hay wagon. Of her tossing hay bales. Of her swinging a hatchet down onto a rooster's neck. He wondered if any of these mothers could do that.

One of the mothers wore shorts over her bathing suit, and her hair was wet. In her car, a white Cadillac convertible, a pair of water skis poked up from the backseat. She waved to King Kenwood, who looked away.

The coach blew his whistle. "That's it for today, boys," he called. "See you tomorrow, ten o'clock sharp."

The boys cheered and raced off toward bicycles and cars.

"I live in the blue house just kitty-corner from the school," the coach said to Billy. "Stop by sometime tomorrow and we'll take a look."

King Kenwood raised an eyebrow in passing. "Extra practice?" he said to Billy.

Billy bit his lower lip.

Tiny Tim popped up beside Billy. "The coach has

to teach Billy how to throw slower," he said to King.

King Kenwood shook his head tiredly at Tim. "You can do better than that."

"How about this?" Tim grinned. He briefly shadowboxed, then darted behind Billy as King tried to grab him.

"Someday, you little shit . . ." King said.

"Nanna nanna na na," Tiny Tim said, peeking around Billy's waist.

"Oh, Archer," called his mother. "Time for your water-skiing lesson."

King turned and headed to the convertible.

"How'd it go today, dear?" his mother asked, putting her arm around his shoulder. King shook it off and climbed into the backseat, where he sat straight-backed.

"Bad day, dear?"

"Very bad, Mrs. Kenwood," Tiny Tim called to her. "He had a very bad day."

She gave Tim a brief stare, then settled in behind the wheel. King sat, looking as stiff as the water skis, and they drove off.

"Thanks a lot," Billy said to Tim.

"Hey—no problem. It's my naturally crazy sense of humor." He bugged out his eyes at Billy.

Billy and Tiny Tim walked uptown after practice.

"So let's do something," Tim said.

Billy shrugged.

"Get a malt at Schinder's."

Billy squinted up at the bank clock. "It's almost

two thirty. I don't know."

Tim followed his gaze, then looked back to Billy. "You can see that?"

"See what?"

"The bank clock."

"Sure," Billy said. It was only four blocks away, a square white clock with black hands. He looked again, squinted slightly this time. "It's twenty-nine minutes to three."

Tim leaned forward and squinted mightily. "Hell, I can't even make out the numbers."

"So you need glasses," Billy said.

"Or maybe you're a robotman of some kind," Tim said, skipping around and then alongside Billy.

Billy let out an exasperated breath.

"Half-man, half-machine—the amazing Billy Baggs."

"You retarded or somethin'? Couldn't you just walk for once?" Billy asked.

"Sure, Billy," Tim said, and held himself down to a skip only every third step.

The Baggs truck was still at the clinic. Billy had a half hour free. "Come on," Tim said, pointing down Main Street to Schinder's. "I'll buy."

"I got my own money," Billy said.

Schinder's had black and red squares of linoleum on the floor, and a long row of stools before a granite soda bar. Rows of glasses were stacked up in front of mirrors, and a COKE sign flashed pinkly in the mirrors and glasses. Across from the till were the magazines and wire cylinders of paperback books. No Magazine

Reading! read a sign. To the rear, pinball machines and dim booths. Old Man Schinder stared up at the TV. It played some afternoon program where men and women argued, then kissed, then argued. Billy's eyes kept going to the TV. They didn't have a TV at home.

Several teenagers, some in orange-and-black letter jackets, turned briefly to look. Tim took a stool, whirled twice and rapped a coin sharply on the counter. Old Man Schinder sighed and turned to the front. "Say there, Tim," he said, his watery old eyes lighting up. "What'll it be today?"

"Whiskey, Mr. Schinder," Tim said. He nodded toward Billy. "Make it a double."

Smiling, the old man began to scoop ice cream into a tin cylinder. His eyes strayed back to the TV as he worked on the malteds: two long squirts of chocolate, three shakes of yellow malt powder, a *glub-glub* of milk. Still watching the TV, he fit the container under the mixer. Metal whined against metal.

"Come on—let's play some pinball," Tim said.

"Don't want to," Billy said. He had already figured out the money. The malted would leave him only forty cents.

They waited at the counter. Tim kept spinning himself around on his stool. Once he ended up backward, facing the magazine rack. "Watch this," he said.

Billy stared as Tim turned back to the counter.

"Any new baseball magazines, Mr. Schinder?" Tim asked.

"There might be, Tim," the old man said. "Take a look."

"Thanks a lot, Mr. Schinder!"

Mr. Schinder turned back to finish the malteds. Tim jerked his head to Billy, who followed him over to the magazine rack. There were more kinds of magazines than Billy had ever seen. Car and baseball and wrestling and weight lifting and hunting and fishing and sailing magazines with colorful, glossy colors. On the bottom row were men's magazines: *Playboy*, *Argosy* and others. Billy stared down at the cover girls. The way they held back their shoulders, the way they arched their backs. He thought of Heather. She could be in a magazine.

"Want a *Playboy*?" Tim whispered.

"No!" Billy said immediately. He looked away quickly, up toward the baseball magazines, where Sandy Koufax was on three covers.

"You want one?" Tim said.

"Huh?"

"A *Playboy*. You want one?"

Billy glanced over his shoulder. "You can't buy one. You got to be twenty-one."

"Who said 'buy'?" Tim whispered. He picked up a Sandy Koufax magazine and pretended to read it. Slowly he rotated his body until he could see Mr. Schinder. When the old man turned away to pour out the malteds, Tim gave a quick tug and ripped the magazine from its cover. He stashed the insides behind some fishing magazines. Then, pretending to tie his shoe, he knelt by the men's magazines. On the way back up, he slipped a *Playboy* inside the Sandy Koufax cover.

Billy's eyes widened. He started to back away—and bumped into a wire cylinder of paperbacks.

Two paperbacks fluttered down and thumped onto the floor.

"Here—boys!" Mr. Schinder called.

Billy quickly replaced the books.

"Sorry, Mr. Schinder," Tim called. He came out holding the Sandy Koufax magazine. Billy followed. Tim was smiling. "I tried my windup and accidentally hit the book rack," he explained.

"No ball playing in here," Mr. Schinder said sternly.

"Sure, Mr. Schinder. I'll buy this and then practice outside."

Mr. Schinder glanced down at the baseball magazine.

Tim held it up, pointed to the price. "One ninety-five, Mr. Schinder," he said. "Here, hold this," he said to Billy, and handed him the magazine.

Billy had no choice. He held it while Tim fished a ten-dollar bill from his pocket.

Mr. Schinder took the money and turned away to ring up the bill for the magazine and the malteds.

Tim laid the magazine on the counter between their malteds.

"Eat up!" Tim said to Billy, and grinned.

Billy finished his malted quickly and headed outside. Tiny Tim drained his glass with a long slurping sound and followed.

"'Bye, Mr. Schinder," Tim called.

The old man smiled and waved.

Outside, on the street, Billy grabbed Tiny Tim by the shirt and hoisted him against a street lamppost. "Why'd you do that?"

"What?" asked Tiny Tim.

"Steal that magazine."

"What magazine?"

"You coulda got me in deep trouble."

"Are you kidding? You're with me. I'm the town pet—everybody trusts me."

Billy dropped Tim, then shook his head disgustedly and began to walk toward Doctors' Clinic.

Tim followed, skipping along. "Besides, Old Man Schinder has a million magazines," he said. "He won't miss one."

Billy ignored him.

"I'm just a crazy kid! A sex maniac. A klepto!" Tiny Tim bugged out his eyes.

"Grow up," Billy said. "And by the way, here's for the malted." Billy took the dollar from his shoe.

"Hey, it's on the house," Tim said.

"Take the dollar and give me my change." Something in the way Billy said it finally got through to Tiny Tim.

His eyes widened. For a moment he looked hurt and frightened. He shrugged. "Okay, Billy—sure!" he said.

"Now beat it; I got to go."

"Where?" Tim asked.

Billy's mother was just coming out the door of Doctors' Clinic. He hurried forward. A man with silvery hair and a white coat stood behind the glass, watching her go. She turned, waved briefly, almost stumbled. Billy saw the man smile at Mavis, then turn away.

"Is that your mom or something?"

"No," Billy said.

"Sure it is," Tim said, and stopped skipping. "She's tall and she's got long arms. She looks just like you." He kept walking with Billy, staring at Mavis.

"Hi, Billy," Mavis called.

Billy didn't wave.

"You must be Mrs. Baggs," Tim said.

"Well, who is this now, a new friend?" Mavis said, smiling down at them.

"Sort of," Billy mumbled.

Tim stared up at her. His mouth fell open a little. "You're so . . . tall—and pretty," he said.

Mavis laughed. "Well, what a little charmer!" She ruffled his hair. For a long moment Tim closed his eyes. Billy had the sudden thought that Tim was going to hug her. Throw his arms around her and hang on. But then Tim opened his eyes again.

"Nice to meet you, ma'am," he said. He turned to Billy. "And here's that baseball magazine you wanted to borrow, Billy."

Billy found himself standing with the stolen magazine in his hands. Tiny Tim skipped off down the street.

Mavis and Billy got into the pickup. Billy sat clutching the magazine. Mavis leaned over for a look. "Sandy Koufax—he's that pitcher?"

Billy swallowed and nodded.

Mavis nodded. "Well, that was certainly nice of Tim," she said as she started the engine.

Billy looked out his window.

"He seems like a nice boy," Mavis added.

"Right," Billy said.

CHAPTER FIFTEEN

O n the west side of town, Mavis slowed the pickup beside Randy Meyers A-1 Cars. Along the highway stretched a shiny row of used cars, or Pre-Owns, as the sign read. Above them stretched a thin plastic rope hung with light bulbs and with little colored pennants that rattled in the breeze. The office was a small log building painted bright orange, with a matching OPEN sign on the door.

Mavis turned and drove in. As she passed the office, Billy saw a man looking out the window. She continued slowly along the row of used cars.

Cadillacs.

Oldsmobiles.

Buicks.

Chevrolets.

Fords.

Toyotas.

Datsuns.

The cars were arranged from new to old. All, even the oldest, were shiny.

Billy remembered something he had heard at the Feedmill: "Never buy a painted woman or a painted tractor." The men had all laughed.

At the far end of the lineup Mavis turned back and drove along, slower this time. About midway she stopped the pickup by a blue 1962 Chevrolet four-door Impala.

"This one," she murmured.

They got out.

The sign in the back window read $750 Good Rubber & Rebuilt Transmission.

Mavis peered inside. Billy did, too.

"Hi, folks!" someone said loudly behind them.

They turned.

"Randy Meyers himself here," the man said, "and that's a real clean unit you're looking at." Randy Meyers was heavyset and balding. His skin was smooth and very tanned. He wore a yellow tie and a wrinkled white shirt. "Let me open up this here Chevy for you."

"We might take a look," Mavis said with as much disinterest as she could muster. She gave Meyers a long look up and down as he flipped through his big circle of keys. "Bingo!" he said, and grinned at them.

Billy looked at Mavis.

She winked.

Meyers bent down and unlocked the door. "This is a local car with loads of economic driving left in it," he said to Mavis. "Yessirree."

She sat inside the car.

Randy Meyers turned to Billy. They stared at each other. "How ya doin', kid," he said. He gave Billy a light punch on the shoulder.

Billy frowned.

Randy Meyers shrugged. His big smile returned as he bent down by the car, close alongside Mavis, as she was about to speak.

"Actual miles, yes ma'am," he said, pointing to the odometer. "Everybody asks it: 'Are these actual miles?' And I don't mind if they do. Because there's no funny business here. Not in a small town like Flint. If I sold you a lemon, why I'd be out of business tomorrow."

"Does it burn oil?" Mavis asked.

"Burn oil? What car doesn't?" Randy said with his wide smile. "Show me a car that doesn't use oil and you've got an exception to the natural laws of internal combustion, physics and geometry."

"How much oil?" Mavis pressed.

Randy Meyers looked hurt. "A quart every thousand."

Mavis looked at Billy.

Who shrugged. That wasn't so bad—if it was true.

"What about the battery?" Mavis asked.

"This battery would turn over a Sherman tank and raise the Titanic—but I jest, of course," Meyers added.

Mavis waited.

"It might go another winter," Meyers said flatly.

Mavis got out and stepped back to look at the car. "Let's take a look under the hood."

Meyers fumbled with the latch, then lifted the hood.

Mavis leaned over. She stared for a moment, then said, "Billy?"

But Billy was already looking. He scanned the engine for oil leaks. Gas-line leaks. For fresh paint. He felt the radiator hose and the belts. He turned the underside of the fan belt to the light. Deep cracks ran across it. "Needs a new fan belt," Billy said.

"What a great kid you've got!" Meyers said. "Such an observant fellow." He clapped Billy hard on the shoulder. Billy rocked on his feet.

"Thank you; yes he is," Mavis said proudly.

"Of course I'd put on a new fan belt for you." Meyers shot a smile Billy's way. Actually it was more like bared teeth.

"Any kind of warranty?" Mavis asked.

"I personally selected this vehicle at a government auction in Fargo," Meyers said. "I've been in the auto business half a decade and believe me, I know a solid unit when I see one."

There was silence.

"The Ford dealership gives sixty days' parts and labor," Billy said to Meyers.

"What a fine son you have, bright fellow with a good memory. He'll go far in this world," Meyers said. He clapped Billy extra hard on the back this time. Billy coughed and stumbled forward a step. "Thirty days' parts and labor is best I can do," Meyers said.

Mavis nodded. "I should test-drive it," she said.

"Of course you should," Meyers said, gesturing toward the open door. "Take it for a free drive, five miles maximum. Sonny," he said to Billy, "maybe you'd like to stay here and have a Coke—on Randy Meyers of course—while your ma takes a test drive?"

"No thanks," Billy said, stepping farther away from Meyers.

"Hop in, then," Mavis said.

And off they drove.

She waited for a truck to pass, then turned onto the highway. The Chevy accelerated smoothly enough. They listened for noises. The engine sounded fine, with no rattle or scrape, and Mavis began to smile. Billy kept listening. There was a faint murmur somewhere, a tiny faraway growling. But maybe it was just the tires. Different tires on a different car. And anyway, the pickup was far louder than this Chevy. He looked over. Mavis was smiling. She put her foot down. The V-8 engine kicked in hard, and they were up to eighty in no time. He heard that faraway whine, again. Mavis did not. She was leaning back and the wind was blowing in her hair. She smiled at him. He decided that the noise meant nothing.

Back at the lot Mavis pulled up by the office. "Thanks," she said to Meyers, handing him the key. "But seven fifty is too steep. I guess we better go, Billy."

They turned away to the pickup.

"Whoa, whoa, whoa!" Meyers called, and trotted up to them. "Someone from out of town, just passing through with seven hundred and fifty dollars in his pocket, then that's the price. But to local folks like yourselves, well, let's talk."

"Five hundred is the best I could do," Mavis said.

"Aaahhhh!" Meyers croaked and clutched at his chest. His heart.

"How much down?" Mavis said.

"Down? Down?" Meyers said, sagging weakly.

"I just got me a job," Mavis said, "and I'll need some time; say six months?"

"A job? Where?" Meyers said, narrowing his eyes.

"At Doctors' Clinic," Mavis said proudly.

"Well of course, of course; why didn't you say so?" he said, beaming again.

"Fifty dollars down," Mavis said.

"Mama mia, I should open up a pizza joint," Meyers said. "But yes—all right—I think we can work out a deal here." He steered Mavis toward the office.

As they worked out the details, Billy took one last look at the car. It sat there, shiny and blue. He stooped and squinted underneath. Under the middle of the car, where the transmission was, there was a fresh drop of something on the gravel. He reached under the car and touched the wet spot. Sniffed his finger. The sharp smell, reddish color of transmission fluid. Inside it were tiny flecks, little brown things. Not metal slivers, but some other kind of chips.

He stood up and thought of heading to the office. Just then Mavis came out holding a paper in her hand.

"Ready, Billy?" she said. Her eyes shone.

He stared at the paper.

"I can pick it up on Friday," she said. "Can you believe it?" She started the pickup's engine and pulled onto the highway. They drove in silence for a while. As they neared home, she reached over and smoothed Billy's hair. "We better not say anything about the car to your pa," she said. "Okay?"

Billy nodded.

In the yard Abner was repairing the mower. A bright spark burned from the welder. As they drove past and parked, he flipped up his mask and shut off the welder. His arms were smudged and his forehead sweaty below the mask.

"Break down?" Mavis said with concern.

"You could say that," Abner said. He stared at them.

Billy saw himself and Mavis through Abner's eyes. Her in her good dress. Billy with his baseball cap, and holding the stolen magazine.

"So how was town today?" he said.

"Fine," Billy and Mavis said quickly in one voice.

CHAPTER SIXTEEN

Tuesday morning, early, Billy watched Mavis walk away. To work. To her first day in town. She walked down the driveway into the raw yellow sunlight to wait for Mrs. Pederson by the road. Mavis had made pancakes and bacon with raspberry syrup for breakfast and a large hot dish for lunch. "All you have to do is turn on the oven at eleven o'clock," she had said.

"What if we forget?" Abner said.

"Ham and scalloped potatoes?" Mavis answered. "You won't."

Now Billy stood on the front steps and watched his mother go. She was dressed up in a skirt and a white blouse. Her rose perfume stayed in his nose. He thought of the pink wild roses that grew along the roads. Their dusty petals that smelled good when he squeezed them. He thought of Robert.

Halfway to the mailbox, his mother turned. She looked black in the sunlight, only an outline of herself. Like she was burning. Like she was on fire. Billy's heart pounded and he felt like he couldn't breathe.

Then she waved.

Quickly Billy waved back.

For a long moment she just stood there. She stared back at the farm. Then—suddenly—she turned and walked on.

Billy headed across the yard to the machine shed. He kicked a stone as he went. He was not going to town this day. He had not even brought up the matter of baseball practice. There were forty acres of hay to bale.

Which reminded him of the magazine. Last night he had hidden it in the hayloft.

Abner was by the tractor, filling it with gasoline. "I'm goin' to check the hayloft," Billy said. "Open up the windows. It'll be hot up there today."

In the loft pigeons cooed and flapped. He paused, looked around. From beneath a hay bale he took out the *Playboy* magazine. Its pages fell open, tan and white and pink. The girls were perfect. He stared at them and felt movement in his crotch. But he kept seeing Heather Erickson. Heather Erickson with her stubby legs and pug nose and her river-bottom smell. She wasn't perfect like these women. But at least she could talk. He took a last look at the *Playboy*, including a look at Sandy Koufax and his high leg kick, then stashed the magazine away and set about his work.

High in the loft were four small windows. Ladders, rough boards nailed to the stud walls, rose up to them. The loft would be cooler still if the big hay door could be let down. As large as the side of a house, the big door was used in the old days—long before Billy was born—when hay was put into the barn loose. Inside the loft, along the peak of the roof, was a single iron track running the length of the barn. A small iron carriage, about the size of a baby buggy, hung on it. Its wheels were rusty and silent.

In the old days, ropes hung down from the carriage. Slings were laid on empty wagons, and loose hay from the field piled on top. Billy's granddad had told him all about it. Horses brought the wagons alongside the barn, and there the carriage ropes were hooked to the slings. The loose hay was then lifted high and carried by the sling deep into the loft. Someone jerked a small trip-rope and the hay fell where it was needed. Then men packed the hay, tramping back and forth to press it down. Loose hay was the reason the old barns were so round and tall. Billy wished they could open the big door someday. Abner said it was a foolish idea, that those days were long gone.

Now Billy crawled steadily up the wall ladder and opened the last of the little windows. Heights did not bother him. Well, a little. But for several years he had been climbing the barn and silo for Abner to open and close vents, windows and doors. When he was back down on the floor, he caught his breath.

He took one more look at the *Playboy*. He unfolded the centerfold girl, Carla. There was a staple in Carla's belly button. She was blond, and her picture was bigger, twice as big as the other ones in the magazine. But the problem still remained: Carla was only twenty-four inches tall. Heather might be stubby, but she wasn't that small. And Heather didn't fold up flat.

"Billy," Abner called.

Billy climbed down. He dropped the magazine in the burner barrel, then turned to sunlight and blue sky and the day's work.

The morning was warm and dry. Cicadas rasped by nine o'clock. A steady breeze had dried the hay windrows of their night dampness, so Abner started up the tractor engine early, at nine thirty. Billy rode the hay wagon as they headed into the field.

Abner kept looking back down the road. Two men were coming to help today. Dale Schwartz was a bachelor mechanic and car jockey who traded work for Abner's lumber and beef. And there was Big Danny Boyer, a giant retarded kid. Not retarded really, just silent. And not a kid, really. Big Danny was in his twenties. He had never said a word in his life. Billy could never remember what was wrong with Big Danny. It was a word like "artistic."

Dale Schwartz was to pick up Big Danny, which might be a problem right off. When Dale Schwartz drank whiskey, he forgot things. And if he did remember to drive over to the Boyer place, Big Danny might or might not get into the truck. Sometimes Big Danny agreed to things. Sometimes Big Danny folded his arms and stood there. It depended. On what, nobody ever knew.

So far today there was no sign of Dale and Danny.

Abner looked down the empty road again and spit.

They baled up the first load alone. Some problems with the twine and the knotter slowed them. Abner kept watching down the road and shaking his head. "A drunk and a retard," he muttered once. "What did I expect?"

At eleven ten Abner looked back and braked the tractor hard. Billy almost tumbled off the wagon.

"The damned hot dish!" he called back to Billy.

Billy leaped off the wagon and ran back to the house.

When he came back into the yard, Dale Schwartz's El Camino pickup was coming up the driveway. Big Danny rode in the rear. His neck and his yellow head rose up over the cab like a thick pine post. He was staring down the road behind him.

Dale Schwartz honked and skidded the truck to a stop. "Hey there, Billy-boy," he called. He was a small, wiry man in his thirties, with brown eyes and dark, wavy hair that was always heavily greased. He had the long sideburns that were in fashion, and one front tooth was missing. Even in the sunniest weather he never wore a cap. He was too proud of his hair, Mavis believed. In the back window was a gun rack and the small, high-caliber varmint rifle he always carried.

"A little late," Dale said. "I saw a badger way out there in the Erickson field. Stopped and drew a bead on him. Two hundred yards—bingo—right in the kisser. He flipped six feet into the air. Good shot; hey, Danny?"

Big Danny stared at Dale.

Dale shrugged. "Well, hop in the back with Weird

Danny and let's get at them bales," he said to Billy.

Billy shot him a dirty look, but he did climb into the back. "Hi, Danny."

Big Danny wore a tattered gray T-shirt, jeans that were a foot too short for his legs, tennis shoes that were burst on the sides, and no gloves. His teeth were filmy yellow. He slept mostly in the barn at home, and never went anywhere. Mavis thought it was criminal, the way his family treated him. Abner said to leave well enough alone. Mavis was always extra nice to Danny, said to treat him like he could hear and think and understand things, but just couldn't put everything together in words. Abner said hard farm work was the best thing for the retarded; it kept them out of town and out of trouble.

Once there had been an incident with Danny at the country fair. Billy had heard only bits and pieces. Something about some girls. Some girls teasing Danny behind the animal barns. Getting him to take down his pants. It was said he had a huge pecker. They screamed when they saw it. Danny went wild and grabbed at one of the girls. Tore her clothes. Something like that. Now Danny had to stay home all the time. He could never go to town again.

Big Danny kept looking back down the road. He was trying to see where he had come from.

"We're gonna bale some hay today, Danny, you and me," Billy said. "And you'll be home in time for supper; how about that?"

Danny blinked and kept staring off in the distance. Skinner trotted behind the truck. "Here, boy,"

Billy whistled. Skinner sped up and made a scrambling leap into the back. He landed in a tangle of legs and tail at their feet.

"I don't want that damn hound scratchin' the paint," Dale shouted back at them.

"He won't," Billy called. Dale muttered something and kept driving.

Big Danny reached down his hand to Skinner.

"That's Skinner," Billy said. "You know Skinner."

Skinner's tail thudded on the truck bed as he leaned his old head against Danny's leg. Big Danny stared down at him. A faint smile came onto his face.

With the extra help, the baling operation began to find its rhythm. Dale and Danny unloaded the first wagonful while Abner and Billy loaded the second. Abner's mood improved, and by twelve thirty he called a break for dinner. They all headed to the house, Dale leading the way, Big Danny bringing up the rear.

"You can wash up in the summer sink," Billy said to Dale and Danny. It was what Mavis would have said. He kept expecting to hear pans rattling in the kitchen. Kept expecting her to look out onto the porch to make sure they were washing up. But the kitchen was silent.

Dale gave the tips of his fingers a brief rinse, then wiped his hand on the towel. Long, dark smudges came away on the white flour sacking. "Too much soap takes out all the natural oil in a person's hands," he explained to Billy. "Then they want to sell you hand lotion. It don't make sense to me."

Billy helped Big Danny wash up. He held Danny's hands and arms in the water. Each hand was as big as a shovel. Dirt and green alfalfa leaves swirled down the drain. Billy made Danny use a bar of Lava soap. Afterward, he climbed up on a stool—Danny was at least six foot six—and took a soapy rag to Big Danny's face. Sometimes Mavis washed Danny's hair and neck and inside his ears. Billy couldn't reach that high, and besides, enough was enough. "Here's the towel, Danny. Go ahead and wipe off."

Danny obeyed.

In the kitchen Billy set the table and brought out the food. The hot dish was bubbling white with potatoes and ham.

"So where's the old lady today?" Dale asked as he sat down.

"Mavis," Abner said, "she's in town today." He glanced at Billy, who said nothing. His mother said Dale was the nosiest man in the county.

"Must be important to be gone on a hay day," Dale said. "Men to cook for and all." He reached first for the hot dish and took an enormous helping.

"We got plenty of food," Abner said. Mavis always said if a woman friend of hers ever got serious about Dale Schwartz, she would personally take her for a long drive and set the woman straight. And if the woman was still interested in him after that, Mavis would take Dale himself for a short drive, tie one of his greasy old car engines to his ankles and drop him in the nearest lake. Dale Schwartz gave her the creeps, she said.

Billy watched him as he ate. His curly black hair. His small sharp chin. His missing tooth. He couldn't figure out why there where so many stories about Dale Schwartz and women. Women young and old. It had to be his shiny El Camino pickup, Billy decided.

"Any bread?" Dale said.

"Billy, get the bread," Abner said. He passed the hot dish to Danny. Danny stared down at his plate. Abner dished him out some.

"Funny that guy don't starve to death," Dale said, watching Danny, all the while chewing noisily himself.

Danny began to eat. He held his fork straight out from the side of his fist. It looked like a toy fork.

"He does all right," Abner said. "Stays home and tends the cows. Don't drink and get into trouble like some."

"I wonder if he's ever had a drink," Dale said, his squinty eyes staring. "Or for that matter . . ."

"I doubt it," Abner said, helping himself to the hot dish. "And it's well enough his kind hasn't. Once they get started, well . . ."

Billy kept eating.

"What'd be worse, I wonder," Dale said. "Go through life tongue-tied or go through life without whiskey and women?"

"I know which one you'd choose," Abner said.

Dale Schwartz grinned, "Trouble with bein' tongue-tied is, you could still have a woman but she wouldn't stay around long." He winked at Billy.

"Let's keep it clean," Abner said, glancing at Billy.

Dale looked across at Danny. "Funny they can't figure out how to loosen up his tongue. . . ."

"Eat up," Abner said. "We got hay to bale."

And bale they did. That afternoon, as sometimes can happen on the farm, things went smoothly. The tractor crawled along the field, its engine humming steadily. The baler's spring-teeth whirled with their high-pitched squeak as they lifted and pulled the hay into the chamber. The big plunger arm drove forward, *boom-plucka, boom-plucka, boom-plucka*. And every twenty beats the twine knotter clattered and slapped, *ratta-ta-tat*, as it made another bale.

Billy and Abner worked in the field. Dale drove the full wagon back to the barn. Big Danny had the hayloft. By midafternoon they had in six loads, or close to six hundred bales.

Billy and Abner waited in the shade of one wagon for Dale to come with an empty one. They had a drink of water, and waited. They added new twine, and waited. But there was still no sign of Dale. "There he comes," Abner muttered finally. Down the lane a cloud of dust rose and the empty wagon clattered.

Dale swung wide and braked hard.

"I'll grease the baler," Abner said to Billy. "You better ride on back with Dale; see how things look." Abner squinted suspiciously at Dale.

Billy hooked on the full wagon, then got in the pickup with Dale. Right away he could smell whiskey.

"Runnin' a little behind, Billy-boy," Dale said,

blinking his eye several times as he squinted through the windshield. He accelerated sharply.

"Take it easy," Billy said. "We got time."

Behind, Billy's carefully stacked bales swayed and leaned.

"Weird Danny, he's a hay-buckin' fool," Dale said. "He don't even step out for a breath of air."

Billy looked toward the barn.

"After lunch, while we was waitin' for the first load, we had ourselves a little nip," Dale said. From beneath the truck's seat he produced a flask of whiskey. "How 'bout you, Billy-boy, a little nip?"

"Watch the gate there," Billy said.

Dale steered them—just barely—between the posts.

"You're what now, fifteen or so?"

"Almost fourteen," Billy said.

"Jesus, you're a big devil."

"And you'd best slow down, else we'll lose some bales."

"I was born to drive," Dale said. "Hay wagons is in my blood; I'm a drivin' fool."

Billy held on to the door handle, and they arrived at the barn without trouble. Billy looked around for Danny.

"He's in the hayloft somewhere," Dale said. "I just keep runnin' the bales up there. Don't hear no complaint from him." Dale laughed so hard, he began to cough and wheeze and spit.

Billy scrambled up the elevator into the loft. Bales rose in a crazy pile, a jumbled cone of green, all the way to the top of the chain. "Danny?" But Danny was nowhere to be seen.

Then Billy saw Danny. Not all of him. Only one foot poking out from beneath the pile. "Danny!" Billy began to tear away the bales. Dale appeared beside him and began to help. They uncovered his legs, then his arms and chest. And finally his head.

"Danny!" Billy tore away the last bales and they dragged him free. Danny was breathing. Luckily the bales, in their jumbled pile, had left an air space. Billy slapped and pinched his cheeks. Danny burped. Billy turned his face away from the whiskey smell.

"I don't know what gets into his kind," Dale said.

"Whiskey, that's what's got into him," Billy said angrily.

"Hey—I was just tryin' to loosen up his tongue a little."

Danny sat up and looked around. When his eyes focused on Dale, they squinted narrowly.

"Well, we better get back to work," Dale said, heading toward the ladder. "He looks okay to me."

"He needs some fresh air," Billy said. "Let's get him down."

They helped Danny down the ladder and then outside. Billy splashed cold water on Danny's face, then gave him a big drink. After a few minutes Danny was back to normal.

"See? No harm done," Dale said. He pointed to the hayloft. "Let's go, Danny-boy, or old Abner will be back here on the warpath."

Danny looked up at the hayloft, then turned back

and folded his arms across his chest.

Dale looked at Billy, then back to Danny. "Hell's bells," he said.

Because Big Danny would not move a step toward the loft.

Billy held back a grin. "Sorry," he said to Dale. He pointed toward the hot, dusty loft. "Guess you'll have to take over."

"Me? I can't take that heat, that dust in the hayloft," Dale said.

"You shoulda thought of that before you gave him the whiskey," Billy said. He was surprised to sound like Abner.

"Don't you talk smart to me, boy," Dale said. He stood up to his full height, which was two inches below Billy's.

Billy met his gaze. "Either you talk to me or you talk to my pa."

Dale's black eyes blazed with anger. Then he backed off. "All right, Billy-boy," he said. "For now." Muttering, he headed up the ladder to the loft.

"Anyway, it's only fair," Billy added.

"Fair? Since when does fair count with retards like Danny?" Dale spit out as he reached the loft. He stood framed in the doorway. "Besides, I doubt Weird Danny knows what to do down there."

Billy thought he saw something like a gleam in Danny's eyes as he stared up at the hayloft door.

"Let's find out," Billy said. "Okay, Danny," he said, and pointed him toward the wagon.

Danny headed straight to the wagon. He plugged

in the cord, then placed a bale on the moving chain. Then another. And another.

"Hey!" Dale said. "Slow down!" He stared at the row of bales heading his way. Billy laughed and turned away to look out at the field. When he looked back he saw a green line of bales flowing up the elevator into the hayloft. The bales looked like a traffic jam of little green cars all heading into the same garage. Billy could not even see daylight between them. From inside the barn he could hear faint and continuous swearing.

CHAPTER SEVENTEEN

The next morning Billy's fingers ached from handling hay-bale twine. His nose was stuffy from hay dust, and black dust watered from the corners of his eyes. But it would be two days before there was more hay to bale. Right now he walked down the driveway with Mavis, carrying his baseball mitt.

They waited by the mailbox and looked down the road. The early morning sunlight was bright. Billy blinked and blinked his eyes. They felt gritty and watery. His arms and legs felt stiff.

"I wish she'd come," Mavis said, glancing at her watch.

"She'll come," Billy said.

Mavis smiled and touched his hair. "When I get that Chevy there'll be no waitin' for nobody. We'll come and go as we please, right?"

Billy grinned. A meadowlark called. He perched on the fence post, and his yellow chest and black throat quivered. They waited. "There she is," Billy said, and pointed.

A brown Ford appeared. It pulled a trail of dust behind. A long way off it began to slow for them.

"She's the penny-pinchingest woman I've ever met," Mavis muttered to Billy. "She lets her car coast to a stop so she doesn't wear out the brakes."

The Ford, its engine silent, passed them by several yards. Mrs. Pederson, a narrow-faced woman with glasses, frowned at Billy as she rolled by.

"Come on," Mavis said to Billy. They hurried toward the car.

"Do you mind if Billy rides along today?" Mavis asked cheerfully. "Some days he has baseball practice."

"I suppose there's room," Mrs. Pederson said. She had a small, pinched mouth.

"Climb in the back, Billy," Mavis said.

Mrs. Pederson started the engine and accelerated as slowly as she had stopped. Her beady eyes stared down the road. "Gas is so expensive nowadays," she said. She made a clucking sound with her tongue. "I try to save as much as I can."

"Things are high all over," Mavis agreed. She winked at Billy.

"I read where every time a person stops and starts a car it costs a dollar," Mrs. Pederson said. She turned to Mavis. "Maybe more."

"It's the big oil companies," Mavis said, sighing like Mrs. Pederson. "They've got us over a barrel."

Mrs. Pederson clucked her tongue again. "I read

about a man in North Dakota. He developed a carburetor that gets two hundred miles to the gallon. Standard Oil bought up the patent and nothing's been heard about it since."

"They're all in cahoots," Mavis replied, mimicking Mrs. Pederson's voice.

Mrs. Pederson turned and raised one eyebrow.

Mavis smiled innocently as she watched the road.

"So how is your garden coming?" Mrs. Pederson said. "Your chickens? I'll be needing my eggs on Friday."

"I'll give her some eggs, all right," Mavis muttered as Mrs. Pederson's car eased away from Doctors' Clinic. "A couple of hard-boiled ones right in the kisser." Mavis straightened, smoothed her skirt and her hair. She reached into her purse. "Here's a sandwich for lunch and a quarter for a soda," she said. "You'll be here at two thirty?"

Billy nodded. She cleaned the corners of his eyes with a finger as Billy tried to lean away.

"My second full day," she said, beaming at Billy.

"Do you like it?" Billy said. As he glanced at the clinic, movement in the window caught his eyes.

"Oh, yes," Mavis said. "One of the nurses doesn't like me for some reason, but the doctors are great. Especially Doctor Lloyd."

"Is that him?" Billy said.

She turned.

A man with a tan face and white hair, the same man Billy had seen before, was looking out the window at them. He wore a white jacket, and a stethoscope hung around his neck.

"Yes," Mavis said. Quickly she turned back to Billy. "That's him."

The doctor waved briefly, then turned back to his chart.

"I got to go," Mavis said. She gave Billy a quick pat on the cheek. "Wish me luck?"

"Luck," Billy said softly. He watched as Mavis hurried up the concrete steps and disappeared inside. She left behind the smell of rose perfume.

First things first. Billy headed past the empty ball field and the quiet school. He walked up to the blue house kitty-corner from the school. At exactly 8:03 A.M. Billy knocked on the door of Coach Anderson's house.

Nothing happened.

He rapped again, louder this time.

As Billy waited, he looked around. It was a one-story house, not large, with an attached garage. A small yard with a low fence and a trimmed hedge. No swing set or children's toys. Some flowers—petunias, geraniums and several other kinds he had never seen before—sat on or hung from a wooden deck.

Everything about the coach's house look organized. Looked done. There were no corrals in need of fencing. No building that needed roofing. No tractor parts or empty fuel and oil barrels here and there. No piles of boards and sawdust. No fields to be baled or plowed. No gopher mounds. A house and a yard like this meant that everything could be kept neat. With time left over. Billy wondered what it would be like to live in a place where there was time left over.

At 8:03 that morning Coach Ozzie Anderson lay in bed with his wife, Sheila. The night before, he had umpired a men's softball game that went sixteen innings. And Sheila, who could not sleep unless he was home, had stayed up practicing a Beethoven piano sonata. She taught piano and occasionally traveled to give concerts in North Dakota and Wisconsin.

They were both in their middle forties and had no children. Not that they hadn't tried. But nowadays they were focused on other things. Sheila had her piano; Ozzie had his coaching and umpiring. They did not talk about having children now. Rather they tried to think of the opposite. Of the benefits of not having children. One pleasure they had, unlike their married friends with kids, was that Ozzie and Sheila could sleep late on summer mornings.

In his dreams, Ozzie kept hearing a thudding sound.

"Ozzie, someone's at the door," Sheila mumbled.

Ozzie groaned. "Paperboy, probably. He'll go away."

The knocking continued. A steady *rap-rap-rap*. *Rap-rap-rap*.

"Ozzie," his wife murmured.

He reached out one big arm to Sheila. She was warm; the bed was warm. He and Sheila could lie in bed another two hours. Who knew what might develop?

Rap-rap-rap.

"Okay—okay!" Ozzie called. He thudded his feet onto the floor. Muttering, he pulled on his bathrobe and went to the front door.

There stood yellow-haired Billy Baggs.

"I come to paint," Billy said.

Billy Baggs, with his squinty blue eyes and crooked teeth, stood there on the steps.

The coach stared a moment. "Billy. I thought it was the paperboy," he said. He scratched his head. He looked once behind him, down the hall.

"Nope. It's me," Billy said.

"Well. Come on in," the coach said.

Billy stepped inside.

"Who is it?" A woman's voice came from the dark part of the house.

"Billy Baggs," the coach called.

"Who?!"

"Billy Baggs, of course!" As the coach winked at Billy the thought passed through his mind that someday everybody would know the name Billy Baggs. The idea passed quickly, like the shadow of a speeding bird, and did not stay with him.

The coach squinted at Billy, then shook his head to clear away the last cobweb of sleep. "It's all right," he called to Sheila. "Go back to sleep."

As the coach spoke to his wife, Billy looked around. The inside of the house had that same neatness. Some fancy blue plates on the kitchen walls. Some pictures of flowers. Some shiny copper kettles hung above the counter, with not a single black burner mark on their bottoms. And no smells. No stewed tomatoes, no potatoes just peeled, no pot roast, no bacon or pancake smell. He wondered if there was any food in this house.

"You had breakfast?" the coach asked.

"Yessir," Billy answered.

"Well, sit there on the stool while I have my coffee," the coach said.

Billy obeyed. He placed his mitt beside him on the counter.

The coach bustled about with a coffee machine. Billy inspected the kitchen as he poured in water, then spooned in brown coffee.

"Missed you yesterday," the coach said.

"Balin'," Billy said.

"About done for the season?"

"Pretty near. Last cuttin' now, another forty acres or so."

"We got a big game coming up," the coach said. "Buckman. Here on Saturday afternoon. Think you can make it?"

"Depends," Billy said.

"On the weather," the coach added. The coffee machine began to gurgle.

Billy smiled.

The coach nodded. While he waited, he stepped outside to look for the newspaper. "Late again," he muttered. "I umpired late last night. Did you happen to catch the Twins and California on TV?"

"We don't have no TV," Billy said.

"Any TV."

"Any," Billy repeated, blushing slightly.

"Okay."

"But I listened to it on the radio in the barn. Twins won, four to two."

The coach smiled. "Fine, fine." He glanced over at Billy. "Ever been to a Twins game?"

"Nope."

The coach poured himself a cup of coffee. "Ever been to Minneapolis?"

Billy shook his head.

"Fargo?"

"Nope."

"Detroit Lakes?"

"Sure," Billy said. "We haul our steers there every fall."

The coach scratched his head. "At the end of the season the team always goes down for a Twins game."

Billy's eye widened.

"We take a bus down and back in one day. An afternoon game. It's pretty cheap, around twenty dollars for everything," the coach said.

Billy looked away. Out the window.

The coach saw Billy's disappointment. He looked at him a moment. "How 'bout you?" he said to Billy.

"Me?"

"You drink coffee?"

"Nossir. Not yet, I guess."

The coach poured a second large cup, added milk, spooned a heap of sugar in after, and shoved it toward Billy. "Now you do."

Billy grinned and put his hands around the warm cup. Its heat felt good on his fingers. The steam felt good in his stuffy nose.

"Sip on that while I get dressed and organized," the coach said. "Then we'll look at the garage."

Billy sat in the quiet, orderly house. It felt like a church. From somewhere down the hallway came the murmur of voices, the coach and his wife. Then the coach crossed into the bathroom, and water began to run. Billy sipped the coffee. It was supposed to wake people up, but he only felt sleepy. While he waited for the coach, he put his head down on his old mitt. Just for a second, that was all. . . .

A few minutes later Coach Ozzie Anderson came down the hallway pulling on a sweatshirt over his big chest. He began to speak, but stopped. There, at the kitchen counter, Billy Baggs sat with his head down. On his old mitt. He was snoring.

The coach walked closer and stared down at him. At the faint brown half-moons under his eyes. At his ears that were none too clean. At his hands, his long fingers that had broken nails and bits of green under them. At his scratched wrists, the little red prick marks from hay bales. He looked at the long ropy muscles in his arms; Billy Baggs had the strongest arms the coach had seen on any young boy.

The coach turned away. Quietly he poured himself

another cup of coffee. By then the newspaper had arrived, so he looked through it. He was careful not to rustle the pages.

He read the headlines.

The world news.

The local news.

He saved the sports section until last. Carefully, he read all the box scores. All the little articles. There was also a sports column by Patrick Rushdie, the sports columnist and general pessimist. Today Rushdie's column was about young baseball players—how few of them ever made it to the major leagues. How Little League coaches perpetuated unrealistic dreams. How few young boys really understood the odds against them: more than 5000 to 1. Coach Ozzie Anderson looked up from his newspaper to stare at Billy Baggs.

Who awoke with a jerk and looked around.

"You must have done some serious baling yesterday," Coach Anderson said. He rattled his paper to a new page.

Billy jumped up and rubbed his eyes. "Sorry . . . I was just . . ."

"Checking your eyelids for holes?" the coach said.

"I g-guess so, yes," Billy stammered.

"Hey, it's all right." The coach laughed. "I needed ten minutes to read the sports section anyway."

Billy nodded.

They headed outside.

"I used to buck hay when I was a kid," the coach said. "So how many bales did you get in?"

"A thousand," Billy said proudly.

"That's a pretty good day," Coach Anderson said, "though I once put up fourteen hundred."

Billy looked up at him skeptically.

"Or was it twelve hundred?" the coach said with a merry glint in his eyes. He walked with Billy along the south side of the garage. They looked up at the trim. "Here it is. Some areas ought to be scraped, I guess," Ozzie said.

"All of it has to be," Billy said decisively, "or else the paint will just peel. Also, we got to find out whether it's oil-base or latex paint."

Ozzie handed Billy the scraper. When the talk turned to work, Billy sounded older than thirteen. Billy climbed up the stepladder and tested the scraper on a board. Paint chips fell away. "It won't take all that long."

"A couple of hours maybe?" the coach said hopefully. "Practice doesn't start until eleven o'clock." He looked back at the house, at his bedroom window, where the shade was still drawn.

"Maybe. Maybe less," Billy said.

"Take your time," the coach said. "I'll check on you in an hour or so." He headed straight back to house.

Inside, the hallway was still dark and silent. Which meant Sheila was still in bed. Which meant he was in luck. Stripping off his sweatshirt, Ozzie slid quietly back under the covers.

Sheila stirred.

The coach put his hand on her warm white shoulder. She burrowed closer into him. "Let me wake up first, honey." she said. "And then if you're in no hurry . . ."

"I'm in no hurry," Ozzie whispered. Outside he could hear steady scraping noises coming from the garage. He hoped they wouldn't make Sheila nervous. She was the kind of woman who liked everything regular. Everything routine. She had delicate nerves and did not like surprises.

Ozzie was not that kind of person—at least he thought he wasn't. But maybe he had changed. Maybe he had become more like her and less like himself. Whoever that was.

He lay there thinking about that. Sometimes he wondered about being an eighth-grade teacher and coach and small-town umpire. Was this all there would be to his life? Was that it for him? His heart beat fast. It always did when he thought about those things.

He looked for a long moment at Sheila, then lay there staring at the ceiling.

Twenty minutes later Sheila woke up. She rolled close to him and opened her eyes. She blinked and smiled. "Hi, there," she murmured. She put her arm across his chest. Ozzie began to forget about everything.

Twenty minutes later, there was a rapping on their bedroom door.

"What!" Sheila cried out, frightened. She jerked

away from Ozzie and dove under the covers.

From beyond the bedroom door came the voice of Billy Baggs. "Done," he said.

Coach Anderson lay back. He shook his head. Then he smiled. Soon he began to laugh, with great guffaws of laughter that echoed off the ceiling.

CHAPTER EIGHTEEN

Billy was drinking a second cup of coffee in the coach's kitchen when the coach's wife, Sheila, came in. She was pretty in a pale, bony way. Her oval face was untanned, and she had dark eyes and a long white neck. Her black hair was cut short, and seemed darker than it ought to be. But it was her hands that caught Billy's eye. Straight, long fingers. Perfect fingernails that shone clear as varnish on white pine. Billy put his own hands behind his back.

"This is Billy Baggs," the coach said. "My wife, Sheila Owens Anderson."

Billy jerked up his chin.

Sheila gave Billy a long stare. Then her gaze fell to the floor. "Please brush off your jeans outside."

Billy vamoosed. He stood just outside the screen door and slapped at his jeans.

"Billy's doing some paint scraping for me," Coach Anderson said.

"I can tell," Sheila said. She picked up a thin

161

broom and began to sweep where Billy had been standing.

"Well," Ozzie said to her, "I guess I'm off to practice."

Billy waited outside the screen door.

Sheila glanced at her watch. "Early, isn't it?"

"Billy's new to the team. I should go through a few things with him."

Sheila looked at the coach for a long moment. Then she turned away and kept sweeping and sweeping. Sweeping up things Billy couldn't see.

"Sheila's not a morning person," the coach explained as they headed toward the garage. He added, "Not like you, Billy." The coach's eyes twinkled.

"I won't come so early next time," Billy said. "It's just that my ma gets here at eight."

"You come whenever you want," the coach said, clapping Billy hard on the back. "Just let me know first." They went through the side door into the garage. It was clean but not so neat. There was a deer head, an eight-point buck hung on the wall and some fishing poles and calendar pictures of Canada. To the left of a tool bench were a hammock, a radio, a small TV and a pile of magazines. Within arm's reach was an old white refrigerator that hummed. "In fact," the coach said, "my garage is always open." He gestured at the hammock, the refrigerator, the TV. "If you ever need a place to hide out from the law . . ."

Billy smiled.

The coach handed Billy a long army duffel bag. It

was heavy and clanked with bats. "Could you carry these? And speaking of Sheila, let me tell you about meeting women."

Billy shouldered the bag.

"First," the coach said, as they set off toward the field, "you don't want to stand there and jerk your chin up and down. Only rubes do that."

Billy blushed and looked down.

"You say, 'Hello. Pleased to meet you, ma'am.'"

Billy nodded. He kicked at a pebble.

"Go ahead, say it."

Billy said it.

"Louder. Like you really are pleased."

"Hello. Pleased to meet you, ma'am!" Billy said.

"Yes—that's it!"

Billy grinned.

"Also if it's a girl, and she's not married, you should say 'Miss.' But then there's the whole Ms. business that's starting." The coach scratched his head. "But that will go away. At least I think so. Best thing, if you have any doubt about what to say to her or anybody, just say, 'Hello—it's a pleasure.'"

Billy nodded.

"Well go ahead," the coach prodded.

"Hello. It's a pleasure!"

"Good. Also, you were right not to shake hands with Sheila," the coach continued. "Really it's women who are supposed to make the first move toward a handshake. You see . . ." As they walked along toward the field, Coach Anderson talked about all kinds of stuff that he called "goodetticut." The word reminded

Billy of "Connecticut." He had never been there, either.

At the field Billy carried the duffel bag down into the empty dugout.

"Rack up those bats," the coach said.

As Billy worked, he looked at the rafters, at the number of nails, at how the dugout was built, at the kids' carving on the wood. He looked around at the empty field.

The coach unlocked a padlock and began tossing out the base bags from a locker. Billy caught them. Felt the hard, dusty canvas squares. Hefted them. "Take these around," the coach ordered. Billy trotted out with the bases. It took him a minute to figure out the hook and ring on first base, and then the others were easy.

On the way back to the dugout, he stopped by the pitcher's mound. He looked at its red hump. Clay and gravel in a flat mound. At the worn area by the dusty white rubber.

"Step up there," the coach said as wheeled out the little machine to run chalk lines. "See what it feels like."

Billy stepped closer but did not go onto the mound.

The coach bent down and poured a small bag of white lime into the open hopper. A small cloud of dust rose. He watched Billy Baggs from the corner of his eye.

Billy looked around once more, then stepped onto the mound. It felt high.

The coach made sure to keep busy adjusting the liner, its settings.

Billy touched a toe to the pitching rubber. He stood there, looking down at home plate. He pretended to throw. He stumbled forward with an awkward step.

"Try pushing off with the other foot, your left one," the coach said, barely looking up from his adjustments.

Billy quickly looked over at the coach. Then he placed his other foot on the rubber. He threw another pretend ball.

Coach Anderson trotted back to the dugout. "Here," he called, and tossed Billy his old mitt, and after it a ball. "I've got plenty of time to run the lines. Let's warm up a little."

Billy stepped down from the mound.

"Go ahead and stay up there," the coach said.

Billy shrugged. And they began to play catch.

Coach Anderson stood in front of home plate. Billy stood on the front of the mound. They lobbed the ball back and forth.

"Nice and easy," the coach said.

After a few minutes the coach said. "Try it from the rubber."

Billy looked uncertainly at the rubber.

"Take your time."

Billy tried a windup, but stumbled off the rubber as he threw. The ball went wide, all the way to the backstop. "That's all right," the coach said as he trotted after the ball.

Billy tried another windup, another pitch. The ball sailed the opposite direction this time.

"Try the set position," the coach said, as he retrieved the ball. "It cuts down on the motion. Less motion, less things to go wrong."

Billy moved back in front of the rubber. Standing sideways, he pushed off and threw. The ball narrowed closer and went *pop!* in the coach's glove.

"Nice," the coach called, and flipped the ball back. "Again. Just hit my glove."

Billy threw straight on this time.

And straight on the next several throws.

"Now you're doing it," the coach said. He backed up a step, crouched on one knee. He held his glove by the other knee over the white plate. "See if you can hit the target."

Billy set his sights on the glove and pushed off again. *Pop!*

"Strike one," the coach called.

Billy grinned. He set. Threw.

"Strike two."

The coach flipped the ball back. "Put something on it this time," he called. "Blow it by him."

Billy rolled the ball in his fingers. He readied himself, then reared back all the way and fired.

The coach did not have time to move. The ball came in a blur of white and hit his glove—a regular fielder's, not a catcher's glove—dead center in the pocket. Dead center on one thin layer of leather and then the skin of his palm: *SAAAAWAAK!*

The coach rocked backward from the blow. His

hand felt as numb as if a dentist had shot it full of Novocain.

"Strike three . . ." he managed to call out. He gritted his teeth. He stood up and flipped the ball back to Billy.

Billy saw the coach flexing his hand. "Was that too hard?" he asked quickly.

Ozzie Anderson stared. He let out a groan that was part laugh—but mostly groan. "It was . . . just right."

Billy got set to throw again.

"That's it for now," the coach said quickly, waving him off. "I have to do an . . . errand. You keep an eye on the equipment. And while you're at it, take a look at the official Little League handbook in the duffel bag. For example, how far is the rubber from home plate? There's a tape measure in there, too." It was an old teacher's trick: to buy some time, ask a question.

"Sixty feet and six inches, maybe," Billy said, "though it don't look that far." He stared toward home plate.

"It doesn't because it isn't," the coach said. "Check it out, and I'll be right back."

Billy found the book and the tape measure as the coach trotted across the park toward the street and the gas station.

Billy began on page one. He read the dimensions of the field, the height of the mound. He looked out at the real field, then took the book and paced off the distance. From home plate to the rubber was exactly forty-six feet. The book was right.

He returned to home plate, checked its measurements: it was seventeen and a half inches wide. The book was right again. He always had imagined home plate was narrower than that. Anybody ought to be able to throw a ball over something seventeen and a half inches wide. He measured the batting box. The base paths.

Then the coach was back. He held a cold can of pop in his left hand, his catching hand, but did not open it. "Hot today," the coach said. There was a shine, a gleam in his eye.

Billy stared as the coach unrolled some white tape, bit off a length and crisscrossed it over the can. And then over the back of his hand. Now he wore a Pepsi coldpack on his palm.

"I'm real sorry," Billy said.

"Get your butt out there and run the chalk lines," the coach said. "I'll tell you how."

By eleven o'clock the other ballplayers began to appear. King Kenwood was one of the first to arrive, in the white convertible. His mother dropped him off. King did not wave good-bye to her. "Hi, Coach," he said. He did not look at Billy as he went off by himself, found a spot on the grass and began his stretch. King Kenwood knew all the exercises. Ones that loosened his legs. Ones that loosened his back. Ones that loosened his stomach muscles.

Other players rode up on their bicycles. Dusty Streeter, who played shortstop, was friendly to Billy.

Butch Redbird, a short, stocky Indian boy who was catcher, came skidding to a stop on a wild-looking bike. The wheels were different-sized. No two parts were the same color. "Hey, man," he said to Billy, and put out a hand.

"Hello. It's a pleasure," Billy said.

Butch stared, then shook hands with Billy. "Groovy," he said. He gave Billy one of those handshakes that went on for a while, the kind black athletes used. Billy had some trouble figuring out when it was over, but he got most of it right.

"That was far out, man, that first day? When you threw in the home-run ball from the Feedmill?" Butch said.

Billy grinned.

"I tagged that sucker out and his eyes looked like golf balls. His mom started to scream liked I'd scalped him or something."

"Hey Butch," King Kenwood called, "warm me up."

"Later," Butch said to Billy. "The King calls."

Billy watch Butch Redbird trot away. He had stubby bowed legs and a big chest. Billy liked him. Abner had a thing about Indians. He called them drunks and welfare cheats. But Butch was as friendly as anybody.

Except, of course, for Tiny Tim Loren. "Hey, Billy!" His high voice trilled right in Billy's ear. Tim had zoomed up on a new, bright-blue bike with knobby tires and straight handlebars.

"Great," Billy muttered.

Tiny Tim hopped off. He let the new bike roll and

crash in the dirt. He didn't look where it fell. "Billy—you're back!"

"So?" Billy said. He stared at the new bike in the dirt, on his guard against a hug or something typically dumb from Tiny Tim.

"So after practice let's do something."

"Like steal somethin'?" Billy said. He caught Tim by the sweatshirt and hoisted him in the air.

"No way, Billy!" Tiny Tim said. "I was just showing off."

Billy let him down.

Slowly.

"Really," Tiny Tim said. "Today we could, like, go to the beach or something."

"Probably not," Billy said.

After warm-ups, they counted off into teams. As usual, King and Nix ended up together. They were number ones. Billy and Tim Loren were number twos. As the count-off continued, Tiny Tim gave Billy the lowdown on the rest of the twos.

"Dusty Streeter is great at shortstop. Rickey Finn and Larry Williams are outfield. Jake 'the Fake' Robertson plays first base and pitches, too."

Jake the Fake was taller than Billy, but skinnier than a yearling colt. He was all legs and arms. "Why do they call him the Fake?"

"You'll see," Tiny Tim said. He went on to finish the lineup, which included Butch Redbird. "Not bad, not bad at all." Tiny Tim said, looking at the twos. "Except for me."

The coach spoke to the two teams. "Okay, we're going to go five innings and then we're done. A big game on Saturday, so don't throw your arms out, all right?" He looked at King Kenwood, who nodded slightly.

The coach looked back at the two teams. He scanned them once. Then twice. "Captains for the day are . . . Doug Nixon and Dusty Streeter."

Dusty Streeter grinned broadly. "Okay, kiddies," he said immediately to his team. The twos groaned.

In the dugout Dusty stood on the bench. "Call out your first choice for positions." He wrote rapidly on a paper on a clipboard as the others shouted their choices. Billy watched Dusty. He seemed so relaxed, like he actually was a coach. Billy could never do that. He wondered where that came from, that kind of confidence. "One at a time, kiddies," Dusty called. After a while things quieted down. Billy had not said anything.

"Third base is open," Dusty said.

"Put Billy there," Tiny Tim said.

The other boys looked at Billy.

"It don't matter to me," Billy said softly.

"The hot corner," Dusty said to Billy. "Third base is yours."

Billy tried not to grin.

"Now the batting lineup. Leading off is . . . Tim Loren."

"No way," Tim moaned.

"Hey—you got a hit off King last time," Dusty said.

Tim shrugged. And smiled.

Dusty went down the list:

RF	Tim Loren
2B	Shawn Howenstein
SS	Dusty Streeter
Catcher	Butch Redbird
1B	Dave Nelson
CF	Ricky Jokela
LF	Curt Hadrava
3B	Billy Baggs
P	Jake Robertson

Billy would bat in the number eight position. In the majors, that was where the two-twenty hitters batted. Billy didn't mind. He was just happy to be here. He listened to Dusty and he watched the other boys. What they said. How they said it. For an instant Billy thought of Robert. But then the thought of Robert faded, and again there were nine boys laughing and shouting in the battered dugout, with its smell of lime and dust and leather baseball gloves. Somebody ripped off a fart, and everybody leaped for cover. There was great laughter.

"Okay—we're the home team," Dusty said.

"All right!" the other boys said.

Billy looked around. He wasn't sure if he should pick up his mitt.

"Home team always gets last at bats," Tim explained to Billy. "And we're gonna need it."

CHAPTER NINETEEN

The twos took the field. Jake the Fake took the mound. He chewed gum, an enormous wad of white bubble gum. His first warm-up pitch bounced in the dirt. His second pitch flew high over Butch's glove. He blew a large bubble, let it pop, then fired the third pitch straight down the pipe.

Billy and the infielders tossed the ball around the horn until Coach Anderson called, "Batter up!"

Doug Nixon led off. He took two balls, then cracked the third pitch into the center-field gap. He slid in with an easy double.

Jim Davis followed with a four-pitch walk.

Two on, no out.

Batting third, King Kenwood took his time getting into the box. He took several hard practice swings. Billy took a step backward on defense. King Kenwood looked like a hard hitter.

On the first pitch King squared around and laid down a bunt. The runners took off. Frozen, Billy stared at the ball; it hopped along slow as a cottontail bunny, then tipped over and died. Billy raced in and Jake galloped over from the mound, but there was no play: base hit.

"Sorry," Billy said.

"Shake it off," Jake muttered. He stood with Billy, blowing a large white bubble and rolling the ball in his finger. He looked at the bases full of runners and scratched his head.

Jake threw three balls to the next batter. None were even close to the strike zone.

Butch Redbird trotted out. He jerked his head to Billy, who joined them at the mound.

"I saw this Camaro in town yesterday," Butch said to Jake.

"What year?" Jake said, brightening.

"Looked like a '67."

"My all-time favorite," Jake breathed.

"It had ten-inch slicks," Butch said. "A 427, headers, the works."

"Four-speed?" Jake said.

"No question."

"Far out!" Jake leaned close to Butch. "Did it?" He circled his finger.

"Total burn-out," Butch said. "Clouds of smoke. Scratch in all four gears. You could smell burned rubber for an hour after."

"Too much," Jake said. He let out a long breath and began to rub up the ball with both hands.

"Hey—play ball out there!" Coach Anderson called.

Butch Redbird winked at Billy as they trotted off the mound. "Total motorhead," he whispered. "Car talk relaxes him. Camaros. Corvettes. Any kind of big-block Chevy."

Jake retook the mound. "Tinted glass?" he called down to Butch.

"Black as a solar eclipse," Butch answered.

Jake checked the runner and went into the set; his pitch was a hard strike at the knees.

As were the next two.

"Stee-rike three," the coach called, and rang up the batter.

Butch gave Billy a thumbs-up sign, and smiled.

The fifth batter stepped in. Bases loaded, one out.

After taking a strike, he smacked the next pitch hard to right field. Tiny Tim Loren made a good try, but the ball dropped just beyond his glove. Three runs scored on the triple.

One out, three runs in.

The next batter flied out to left field. The runner tagged and scored.

The last batter lined hard to short. Dusty Streeter made a clean catch and hard throw to end the half inning. Score: four to nothing.

"Okay, kiddies, we better get some hits," Dusty called.

Tiny Tim struck out on three pitches.

Shawn Howenstein singled.

Dusty Streeter hit into a double play and chewed himself out all the way back to the dugout. "Language," Coach Anderson warned. And suddenly the twos were in the field again.

Billy stared at King Kenwood as he trotted by. King had thrown only six pitches that inning.

In the top of the second Jake the Fake blew a large bubble, then struck the first batter.

Walked the next two, including Nix Nixon.

Got Jim Davis to fly out.

Then he grooved a fat pitch to King Kenwood. *WHACK!*

Billy leaped like a deer, but the line drive was over his head, a rising shot that cleared—just barely—the left field wall. A three-run homer!

King took a long time trotting around the bases. Billy made sure not to look at him as he came by third.

The next batter grounded out.

Score: Eight to nothing.

"Okay, girls, it's time!" Dusty Streeter called to his team.

Leading off in the bottom of the second inning, Butch Redbird doubled.

Dave Nelson walked.

Ricky Jokela reached first on an error, which loaded the bases. Butch was on third.

Curt Hadrava flied out to center, bringing Butch home.

And Billy Baggs came to the plate. He touched the plate with his bat and squinted out at King Kenwood. His eyes still felt red from the hay dust; his arms ached. The bat felt heavy. The first pitch was outside and he nicked it foul.

"Swing at strikes," the coach said.

The second pitch was a called strike.

Billy waited. The third pitch he popped up high in the infield. "Batter is out," the coach called. King Kenwood made the catch anyway, and then trotted off the mound.

Billy stared briefly at the coach, then headed to the dugout to get his glove. "Why was I out before he caught it?" Billy said to Tiny Tim.

Coach Anderson overheard Billy. "Infield fly—check the rule book," he said.

Score: Eight to one.

"Shake it off," Butch Redbird said as Billy trotted past on his way to third base.

In the third inning Jake the Fake found his groove. He struck out the first two batters. The third batter pulled a hard grounder toward third base. Billy dove and knocked it down. From his knees in foul territory he threw a strike to first base to nip the runner. His team cheered. Jake the Fake gave Billy a thumbs-up sign and grinned as he jogged off the mound.

Coach Anderson stared down at Billy Baggs. He had never seen that play in summer baseball, not a throw from the knees from beyond deep third. As Billy trotted past, the coach made sure to act casual. "Way to knock the ball down, Billy."

In the bottom of the third inning, Jake the Fake led off. He batted left-handed. He had a long, low swing that came nowhere near King's fastballs. After three of them Jake was gone.

Tiny Tim struck out.

Shawn Howenstein, the butcher's kid, chopped a high bouncer over King Kenwood's head and beat it out for an infield single.

Dusty Streeter stepped up. King threw three fastballs, all high. King stepped off the mound and rubbed up the ball. Billy watched him closely. He stepped back on and threw two strikes. They were slower, and looked like hitter's pitches, but Dusty was taking all the way. The sixth pitch was just low. A walk. King spit and turned his back to the plate. He stared out at center field. Billy thought back to the second inning when King had walked Dave Nelson. It was the same deal. The same sequence. When King was in danger of giving up a walk, he threw a fat pitch or two to get back even in the count.

Butch Redbird took the first pitch to the left-field wall. But the fielder was playing him deep, and made the catch at the Randy Meyers A-1 Cars sign.

One hit. No runs. Score after three: Eight to one.

In the top of the fourth, Jake the Fake popped his gum and blew two fastball strikes by Nix. But then Nix dropped a bloop single into left, and rolled all the way to third on an overthrow.

Billy held Nix close to third.

"Eight to one, Rag Baggs," Nix said as he caught his breath.

Billy said nothing.

"Great pop fly, by the way."

Billy focused on the batter.

"And did I tell you I like your glove?"

As Billy looked angrily at Nix, Jim Davis cracked a grounder to third. With a late jump, Billy still fielded the ball. Nix broke toward home. Billy fired the ball to Butch Redbird. The ball popped into Butch Redbird's glove as Nix turned and trotted back to third.

A fake move home.

Billy fell for it. And Butch Redbird had no play anywhere: Jim Davis was safe at first and Nix at third.

"Nice play, Rag Baggs," Nix whispered.

Billy bit his lip.

King Kenwood stepped up.

Jake, popping his gum faster now, walked King on four pitches. That meant bases loaded with two out.

Jake looked over at Billy, then signaled for Butch and Billy to join him at the mound. They trotted out.

"I got an idea," Jake said.

"Scam time," Butch said. "But we're gonna need something new."

"Who's the Big Daddy of all trickmeisters?" Jake said, pretending to have hurt feelings. "Who's the Big Bopper of baseball bamboozle?"

"You are, my son, you are," Butch said.

Billy wondered what in the world they were talking about.

"Here's the deal," Jake whispered. "Baggs, you're new. No one is gonna suspect you of anything. Plus that old glove of yours can't hide the ball anyway." He explained the trick.

Billy grinned, and Butch whistled softly. "Dastardly. Devious. Son, you'll make a great criminal someday."

"Thank you, Father, thank you," Jake said.

"Hey you guys, play ball out there," the coach called.

And they began the scam.

Jake blew a large bubble, then bent down as if to check his shoe. His bubble was a thick white one. Butch slipped the ball to Billy, who pinched it under his armpit. And Jake, in a smooth motion, wiping his face, spit the gum bubble into his cupped hand. In his palm the bubble was white and round. Well, a little droopy, but white and almost round.

Billy trotted back to third.

"You guys better figure out something besides the old hidden ball trick," Nixon said, still standing on the bag.

Billy shrugged and held out his mitt. It was empty. Nixon squinted back at the mound. At Jake's hand.

The white gum bubble drooped but still was white and humped in his hand.

Nix looked once more at Billy, then took his lead.

Butch Redbird nodded. And Billy stepped over to Nix. "How about a new hidden ball trick then?"

Nix's eyes bugged as the ball dropped from Billy's armpit into his glove. Nix, cut off from third, broke toward home. Billy did not let go of the ball this time. Nix faked the run, then had to go home when Billy didn't throw. He was fast, but Billy caught him halfway and tagged him out with a hard sweep across the back. Nix went sprawling in the dust.

"He's out of there!" Coach Anderson called with a swoop of his arm.

Billy's team cheered.

Nix jumped up and went for Billy, raining punches. Billy gave as good as he got, until Butch Redbird leaped between them.

Coach Anderson was there a second later. "Let's play *ball*, all right, boys?"

They glared at each other, then turned away. And the coach trotted off.

Nix scowled at Billy and dusted himself off. "I'll get you for this," he muttered to Billy. "Someday . . ."

King filed out, and the next batter fanned to end the inning.

In the bottom of the fourth, Dave Nelson reached first on an infield error.

Ricky Jokela walked.

Curt Hadrava laid down a sacrifice bunt, but the first baseman dropped the ball. Bases loaded, nobody out.

King Kenwood stepped off the mound and stared out at center field as he rubbed up the ball.

And Billy Baggs stepped up to the plate.

King took a long time getting back to the rubber. Billy looked around the bases. His hand began to sweat. He knew the runners were expecting a hit. Expecting something from him.

King stepped off again and called time. He bent over to tie his shoelace, which looked already tied.

"Play ball," the coach called.

King stepped back onto the rubber and glared down at Billy.

Billy swung hard at the ball, which floated toward the plate. Billy was already through with his swing by the time the off-speed pitch reached him. Strike one.

The second pitch was a low, hard fastball. Billy swung again and fouled it off. Count: 0 and 2.

Billy swallowed and stepped back in.

The next pitch was another foul ball.

And so was the next.

And the next.

And the next.

And the next.

And the next.

And the next.

And the next.

The field went silent. The players watched the matchup between King and Billy. King threw fast and slow. He threw high and low. They were all strikes.

Billy kept lacing them foul. Two foul balls soared high toward left field, curving just foul. Another few inches and they would have been homers.

The tenth pitch was a dead center over the plate. It floated in fat and white and Billy tried to kill it. Instead, he struck out.

Whiffed.

Fanned.

Died.

Billy stood there. He stared at his bat. He couldn't

believe he had missed that one. The base runners trotted off the field to get their gloves.

King Kenwood passed. He looked straight at Billy. Billy glared at him.

Coach Anderson smiled.

The fifth inning passed quickly. Jake the Fake pitched well. Three up and three down.

In the bottom of the fifth, Billy's team managed three runs off a tiring King Kenwood, but they still came up short.

"That's it for today," Coach Anderson called.

Final score: Eight to four.

As the boys dispersed, King Kenwood passed Billy Baggs. He paused. "Nice at bat in the fourth."

"Sure," Billy said.

King shrugged and moved on.

Coach Anderson smiled. Baggs, Kenwood, Redbird. If he could keep those three together he might have something. And there were Dusty Streeter, Doug Nixon, Jake Robertson and the others. Here, possibly, was a real team. The kind that in a few years could— But he stopped himself. Such thinking was sure to bring bad luck.

On the way home Ozzie Anderson went his usual route past the middle school. He walked slowly after practice. Today, as always, he was in no hurry to get home. Sometimes he stopped by his office. He liked it when the school was empty. Sometimes he sat in his office without the lights on and looked out the window. His view, from the second floor, was through the elm trees and across the street. There he could see his own house. Sometimes Sheila worked in her small square of a flower bed. And beyond his house, cars passed down the main highway. Cars going somewhere. Sometimes he sat there for a long time, thinking about things.

Today the school doors were propped open. A tidy trailer with KEN'S DRYWALL AND INTERIOR PAINTING on it sat on the lawn. Somewhere inside the school a radio played.

Ozzie looked up at the old school as he walked along. At its chipped yellow brick. At its blank windows. All the colored posters from last school year were down. The windows were ready for next month's students. He thought about the many hours, the many weeks, months and years he had spent in those classrooms.

He meant to walk on, but instead turned up the granite steps. They were bowed and curved from use. He wondered how many times his own shoes had touched the stones. How much of the wear was from his own feet.

The foyer was dim and cool. Trophies glinted dully in the case by the gymnasium door. He walked closer. The Flint trophy case was not large. A couple of dozen plaques and little statues behind the dusty glass, that was all. Their wood was darkened with age, the brass smoky and tarnished. There had been no new trophies for a long time.

Ozzie stepped closer to the glass. He leaned down to peer at the bottom shelf. There it was, one of the larger trophies. It had a dusty old miniature baseball on top. THIRD PLACE, MINNESOTA STATE CHAMPIONSHIP TOURNAMENT, 1940. Engraved on its side was a list of names. The names were in alphabetical order, starting with Anderson, Oswald—Pitcher.

CHAPTER TWENTY

After scrimmage Tiny Tim tagged along with Billy. "What say we hit the beach and check out the chicks?"

"Can't," Billy said, trudging along.

"Why not?"

"Got to get a physical."

"Oh, man," Tim groaned.

Billy spit. "Coach says I have to have it. League rules, insurance or somethin'."

"I thought everybody already had a physical," Tim said.

"Not me." Billy kicked a Coke can. It clattered across the street. "I ain't never had one."

"In your life?" Tim asked.

"Nope."

"Really?"

"I ain't never even been in a hospital either, except . . ."

"Except when?"

"Nothin'." Billy stopped talking. He glanced up the street at the clinic. At its square brick front. There were windows along the side, the shades pulled all the way down. He thought of Robert. How crumpled he had been. How deep those disk cuts. How the dirt took all his brother's blood like a giant sponge and left him with none at all. How Robert looked somewhat better, later, in the hospital basement. There in the pale lights his face was all right. His face had not been touched. With the sheet over his body his face looked just fine. Just fine, like he could—

"Hey, a physical's no big deal," Tim said, looking closely at Billy's face.

Billy shrugged.

Tiny Tim grinned. "Of course there's the needles. And then there's the butt reamer when they check you for hemorrhoids, and then—"

"Shit!" Billy said, stopping in his tracks, his eyes gone wide as hen eggs.

Tim hooted with laughter, nearly falling off his bike.

"Sure, right," Billy said, walking on again.

"Really all you got to remember is to turn your head when he asks you to cough." Tim said.

"Cough?" Billy said. "I ain't got a cold."

Tiny Tim laughed louder still. "You'll see," he shouted as he sped off on his bike. "You'll see."

Billy watched him go. When Tim was out of sight, Billy squared his shoulders, took a breath, and turned toward the clinic steps.

Inside Doctors' Clinic the air was cool and had a thin, sharp odor, a little like the smell of the chemicals at the Feedmill. In the waiting room faces turned toward Billy. There was a fat woman in a purple dress as big as a tent. She was holding a baby that looked like a pumpkin. There was something wrong with its color. Next to the fat woman was a skinny old man. He had a face as narrow as a crow's, and he dozed with his head tipped back. Billy could see into his mouth; his false teeth were loose and hung to the side. Across from the old man were two pregnant women. They sat together, fingers laced across their bellies.

"Good afternoon," Mavis said. She looked up from behind the counter in front of a narrow office area. She had her own desk. There was her name, engraved on a plastic strip: MAVIS BAGGS. It faced the front so that everyone who came in could see it. She beamed at Billy and stood up.

"Hi, Ma!" he said.

She frowned. "How was practice?" she said softly.

"Okay," Billy said more softly. He looked behind him at the waiting room. The fat woman stared at Billy and Mavis.

"You're here for your physical, I believe," Mavis said more loudly. "A two-thirty appointment with Doctor Lloyd. Let's look in the book to make sure."

Billy stared at her. His mother's voice sounded strange, like she was talking to someone else. Of course he was scheduled for two thirty; they both knew that.

"Here we are," Mavis said. She whispered to Billy, "It's important to be professional at all times."

Billy nodded. "Right," he whispered back.

"Please take a seat. Doctor Lloyd will be with you shortly."

Billy headed for a chair, glancing over his shoulder at Mavis before he sat down.

He found the seat farthest from the fat lady and her sick baby. The fat lady kept her beady eyes on him. Billy reached for a magazine. It was a *Cosmopolitan*. The fat lady narrowed her eyes. Billy swallowed and chose another magazine. This time it was a thick, sticky-paged *National Geographic*. He forced himself to look through an article on seals in Antarctica. He did not like reading.

The old man snored.

The pregnant women told each other stories of water retention, swollen ankles and gas.

Billy was on his third article when someone called his name.

He stood up.

A nurse waited at the swinging doors. She was short and wore all white and her face was pale. Mavis came over. She was a foot taller and looked twice as strong as the nurse. Billy sometimes forgot how tall Mavis really was. He usually only saw her outdoors or around Abner.

"Please accompany Nurse Klein," Mavis said to Billy in her professional voice.

The fat lady checked her watch and said loudly to Mavis, "How's come he's goin' in already? Me and little Darla been here an hour."

"Mr. Baggs has a two-thirty appointment," Mavis said. "We always try to keep our appointments. Drop-ins we see as quickly as possible."

"I don't suppose it helps to be related." The fat lady snorted. She glared at Billy.

Mavis swung around. "Not in the least," she said, "so just keep your damn shorts on."

The fat lady drew back in the chair like she had been snakebit.

Nurse Klein widened her eyes and stared at Mavis.

Mavis smiled pleasantly at both of them, then returned to her desk.

"This way," the nurse said to Billy.

In the little room Nurse Klein said, "Go ahead and take off your clothes. You can slip into this, and I'll be right back."

Billy waited until she left. He stared at the little sheet with strings on it. As he undressed he kept his eyes on the door. He tried the sheet on one way, but that left his hind end bare.

He tried it on another way, but that left him naked in front. He hunched his shoulders against the cold and tried to adjust the gown. Finally he tied it on sideways. That way, only one hip was bare. The hip farther away from the door.

He sat on the plastic-covered table and waited. The plastic stuck to his butt.

He could hear murmuring in the hall. He heard someone say "Mavis." It sounded like Nurse Klein was talking to another nurse about Ma. Billy tried to listen, but a baby began crying somewhere farther down the hall.

He looked around the room. At the glass jar full of cotton balls. They looked like popcorn. At the stainless-steel tray with some fancy-looking pliers. At the needles.

To take his mind off things, he looked at the ceiling. This was worse. On the ceiling was a small brown spray of dried blood. Billy knew blood when he saw it. That clearly was dried blood on the ceiling.

He slid to the far end of the padded bench. His heart beat fast. How could blood get on the ceiling? What went on in these rooms? He looked at the window. At its lock. Not really a lock, just a fastener. He looked over at his clothes on the chair.

But suddenly the door swung open with a *bang*. Nurse Klein homed in on him with some kind of pump and strap. Before Billy could move, she slapped it around his arm.

He squinted as she pumped on a little rubber ball.

"Sit still; breathe normally," she said.

The band tightened like a noose around his arm. His heart pounded.

Nurse Klein looked at the wall clock as she let the air hiss out. She counted to herself. She stared briefly at Billy, then ripped the band loose.

"Now stand on the scale."

Billy did.

The nurse moved the weight, then stretched up to lower a thin steel bar onto his head.

"Seventy inches, one hundred thirty-one pounds,"

she murmured as she wrote. Then she disappeared back through the door.

Billy sat back on his table and chafed his arm. He stared out the window. At his clothes.

Suddenly the door thudded open again. Doctor Lloyd strode into the room. He looked just like a doctor should, with his fine, sharp nose and mostly-white hair. He was reading a chart as he came.

"Good afternoon, Mister Baggs."

Billy stared at the doctor. He swallowed. "Hello it's a pleasure," he said rapidly.

The doctor paused to smile. "Well yes, it is."

His gray eyes met Billy's, and he held out his hand. The doctor had white, firm hands that matched the bones in his nose, and a good firm handshake.

Nurse Klein came in.

Her again.

Billy tugged his gown closer toward his knees.

Doctor Lloyd rinsed his hands in the little sink. Nurse Klein was ready with a towel. "Let's see," he said, leaning over to look again at the chart. "A sports physical today?"

Billy swallowed and nodded.

"Don't be anxious; it won't hurt."

Billy managed a thin-lipped smile. Doctor Lloyd had good, straight teeth and white hands and clean fingernails. Billy kept looking at his hands. He thought of the coach's wife, of her hands. It came to him that there were two types of people in the world: people with rough hands and people with smooth hands.

"Open your mouth wide."

Billy opened his mouth.

Dr. Lloyd put a broad, dry Popsicle stick on his tongue. Billy gagged.

"Fine. Swing around."

Eye on Nurse Klein, Billy rotated partway. The doctor put the cold steel eyeball of his stethoscope on Billy's back. He began rapping up and down with a little rubber hammer.

"Fine. Now your knees."

Billy stared down as the doctor tapped his kneecap with the hammer. Billy's leg shot out. His bare foot nearly hit Nurse Klein.

The doctor smiled. "Let's try that again."

Billy's other leg shot out. "Excellent!" the doctor said. He smiled again.

"Now stand up and bend over."

Billy did so, shutting his eyes.

He heard the doctor snap on a rubber glove. Nurse Klein was ready with a tube of Vaseline. Squinting, Billy saw the doctor take some on a finger. Reach down behind him.

"Ahh!" Billy said.

"A bit uncomfortable, it's true," the doctor said, "but very important to check the colon on occasion."

Billy gritted his teeth.

Finally Doctor Lloyd withdrew his finger and snapped off the rubber glove. "Now stand up and turn your head to the side."

Billy coughed sharply as he felt where the doctor's hand was.

"Again, please."

"Huh?"

"Cough again, please."

Billy repeated.

"And there we have it!" the doctor said. "All done."

Billy let out a breath.

The doctor sat a moment and scribbled something on a chart. "Any problems with high blood pressure in your family?"

"I don't think so."

"Yours was rather high today, but often that's anxiety-related, especially since this is your first visit here." He scribbled something more on the chart. "I'll have your mother check it at home when you're relaxed, all right?"

Billy smiled fully for the first time.

Doctor Lloyd squinted his gray eyes at Billy, then reached out to Billy's face. His hand squeezed open Billy's jaw. He stared at Billy's teeth like Billy was a horse or some farm animal, but somehow Billy didn't mind. "Have you thought of orthodontia?"

"Huh?" Billy asked, puzzled.

"Orthodontia. Having your teeth straightened. Braces."

"No," Billy said quickly. "I ain't ever thought of that."

"I'll mention it to your mother," Doctor Lloyd said. He smiled. "But otherwise, you're in fine shape, Billy. You've had all your innoculations in school. Any questions?"

Billy was silent.

"Good day, then." And with that Dr. Lloyd was gone, disappearing through the doorway as smoothly as he had come.

Mavis was in her office when Billy came out. Doctor Lloyd was there, too, and Mavis was holding one of those blood pressure straps.

"The doctor says you're in fine shape," she said.

"And I *did* mention orthodontia to your mother," Dr. Lloyd said.

Billy split for the door. "See you at four thirty," he called back to Mavis. Behind him he heard Mavis and Doctor Lloyd laugh.

A river ran through town, and at the municipal beach Billy walked slowly up to the changing house. It was a square fieldstone building with a sign over the door: WPA, 1932. A sidewalk ran from it down to the beach. The beach was grass, beaten down by the summer's wear; then sand; then a concrete platform and a diving board. A short lifeguard tower poked up from the sand and a tanned teacher sat slumped in its chair. A bunch of town kids fooled around on the platform, laughing, shouting, cannonballing into the river. Water sprayed and fell back. Girls and boys swimming together. Billy stopped and leaned against the cool stone side of the building, in the shade. From a distance he watched the town kids.

"No running," the lifeguard droned through his megaphone.

The chasing and cannonballing slowed slightly.

Down and to the right was a sand area with mothers and their kids. The toddlers shrieked and flapped at the water. The mothers dozed. Some of them lay with their bathing-suit straps off their shoulders and their legs spread. Some of them were very tan.

Back at the platform he saw some girls from school. Sarah Jenkins, a cheerleader. She was short and brown-haired and wore a two-piece red suit. Suzy Langen, a blonde with a ponytail, was a foot taller than any of the boys. And two feet taller than Tiny Tim Loren.

Tim raced off the diving board, flipped once, curled into a ball and splatted himself between two girls in the water. They screamed and pushed water at him. Suzy Langen walked away, toward her blue-and-white towel on the grass. She tilted her head to the side and squeezed river water from her ponytail. She used long, milking strokes. Water ran from her hand down her brown arm and dripped off her elbow. It sparkled in the sunlight. Then she sat down on the towel and tilted back her shoulders and throat to catch the sun. Billy swallowed. He watched her for a long time.

Back by the diving platform, everybody was in the water now, paddling around, playing water tag, calling out to each other. Tiny Tim was a good swimmer. Disappearing, surfacing ten feet away. Disappearing again. Racing out to cannonball again and again.

And of course he spotted Billy. "Hey—Billy! Come on in!" he called, treading water.

Billy waved.

The other town kids, including Suzy Langen, turned to look. When she saw Billy there in the shadow of the building, she hitched up her bathing-suit top, made a face and turned her back on him.

"Come on, Billy!" Tim shouted.

Billy shook his head "No," then turned back up to town.

He walked slowly to Main Street. He still had an hour and a half to kill. He stopped in front of Rod's Sporting Goods to look at the fish. Tourists brought their fish in to be weighed and displayed. Today there was an eighteen-pound northern pike and a four-pound bass. They lay there, eyes open, staring, slumped and shiny on the ice blocks.

Walking on, he stopped at the Dairy Freeze and bought a dime cone. He leaned against a lamppost to eat it. By the curb was a farm pickup with an old man and his wife sitting in it. Both wore caps. They slowly licked at their cones. Dime cones. They watched every car that passed. Every person who came by. They licked their cones, trying to make them last. Billy walked on.

Farther down the street, a farmer came out of a hardware store. He carried a length of chain. He wore coveralls and a cap and his hands were black from old grease and oil. Billy thought of the doctor's hands, their whiteness. The farmer nodded to Billy. "How you doin' there, Baggs?" he said. Billy remembered him then, from the Feedmill.

"Okay," he said.

"Your old man around?" The farmer looked down the street.

"Nope," Billy said. The farmer moved on. Billy was glad.

For the next hour he drifted on Main Street. There were quite a few tourists, mostly women and girls. They were in from the resorts to shop. Several girls in white shorts and tennis shoes went into the dime store. Billy followed them. Inside, he watched them from across the aisle. They turned his way. He pretended to look at greeting cards.

The girls passed him without a glance. He smelled their perfume. A fruity, strawberry scent hung in the air. He closed his eyes. He tried to imagine where those girls lived. He saw big, catalogue houses. In the suburbs. Minneapolis or Chicago. He thought of Heather. Her muddy, river-water smell. He thought of where she lived, a trailer house parked in the pines. Opening his eyes, he looked around for the tourist girls, but they were gone.

CHAPTER TWENTY-ONE

At four thirty, Billy and Mavis caught their ride home with Mrs. Pederson. Who went on about the big oil companies.

About the Rockefellers.

About the price of bacon.

At the mailbox, Billy's feet hit gravel before the car stopped coasting. Mavis got out. She shook her head as she watched the Ford ease away down the road. "Two more days of her, Billy, then we're free."

In the yard Billy saw the bright white spark from the welder. Abner was hunched over the light, working on the hay mower. He had his welder's hood on. They walked over to him. He heard them and flipped up his hood.

"Break down again?" Mavis said.

Abner's face was hot and streaked with a spot of welder soot. He looked at them. At their clean clothes.

"I'd still be mowin' if it wasn't for the gopher mounds."

"I was figurin' on settin' some traps tonight," Billy said quickly.

"See that you do," Abner said, and flipped down his hood.

After milking and supper, Billy took his sack of gopher traps and found Abner in the machine shed. "I thought I'd go all the way out back. Can I take the tractor?"

Abner squinted.

"I could cover more ground that way," Billy said.

"Plenty of damn gophers out there," Abner muttered. "All right." He limped to the tractor and unscrewed the gas cap. He peered in. "Half full. And don't be drivin' all over. Gas costs money, you know."

"Yessir," Billy said.

He climbed aboard the little tractor and started the engine. He drove carefully down the lane, making sure he didn't look back. Abner would be watching. When the lane curved out of sight from the farm buildings, he shifted into fourth gear and carefully opened the throttle. Moving across the empty hayfield, Billy swung past the rock pile, where he tossed his bag of traps. Then he drove straight to the road gate.

He opened the gate, drove the tractor onto the gravel, then got out to close the gate behind him. With his boots he scuffed out the fresh tractor tracks. Then he put the tractor in fifth gear and headed down the county road.

The Erickson place was carved out of the jack pines. A two-acre cleared space was filled with a mobile home, a homemade barn, a corral and a bunch of old cars and snowmobiles with weeds and grass growing up around them. Buster Erickson had run off with a woman whose house he had painted. No building on the Erickson place had ever felt a paintbrush. And likely wouldn't, now that Heather's mother had to work two shifts at the nursing home in town.

Gina spotted Billy and raced out to the road. He braked to a stop but left the engine running.

"Where you goin'?" Gina called.

"Nowhere," Billy said. He looked beyond Gina to the house.

"Heather's pickin' peas in the back garden," Gina said.

Billy saw Heather stand up in the garden and look toward the road. She fluffed up her hair. In the sunlight it flamed red. Billy looked back at Gina. "So," he said.

"So she can't come along. But I can."

"Come along where?" Billy said, and spit.

"Wherever you're goin'."

Heather came over to the fence. She had on short shorts and a smudged white T-shirt. She carried a plastic ice-cream pail half full of pea pods, and she was smoking a cigarette. She leaned against the fence post. "Well, if it ain't the long-lost Billy Baggs."

He looked off toward the tree, then back.

"So where're you and your Cadillac goin'?"

"Swimmin'. Maybe."

"You goin' by Bob's Barn?" Heather said, suddenly interested. "I could use some cigarettes."

Billy shrugged. "I don't know." Bob's Barn was a combination tavern, gas station and grocery store. It was at least three miles beyond the river.

"If I come swimmin', you can take me there," Heather said.

"You're supposed to pick peas," Gina said.

Heather stared at Gina. She put the cigarette back in her mouth. Then, in a quick swing of her arms, she emptied her pail. Green pea pods soared and caught the light, then rained down green and glowing over Gina and Billy and the tractor.

"I'm tellin'!" Gina said.

Heather turned to the farmyard and shouted. "Gina's tellin'!" Her voice echoed among the silent buildings.

With Gina and Heather perched on the low drawbar behind, Billy drove the tractor toward the river. "Hang on," Billy warned Gina.

"You fall, you'll skin your tits off," Heather added. "Not that we'd notice any difference."

"Look," Gina said. She held up both arms, like she was flying.

"Cut it out!" Billy shouted instantly.

"Don't have a shit fit," Gina said, pouting.

"Don't look at her," Heather said to Billy, leaning close and holding on to Billy. "She's so immature."

Billy drove around a bend.

"Look!" Gina shrieked, pointing toward the woods. "Look!"

By the side of the road, just inside the woods, was Danny Boyer. He was crouched behind some brush.

"It's Weird Danny!" Gina and Heather screamed. They waved wildly and pumped their arms up and down.

"Cut it out," Billy said sharply.

The two girls kept shouting at Danny.

Billy slowed the tractor. "Cut it out or I'll stop!"

The girls stopped shrieking immediately. They looked over their shoulders at Danny, who peeked out from behind a tree.

"What's he doin'?" Gina said.

"He's out for a walk," Billy said.

"Why is he hidin'?"

"Maybe he just wants to be left alone," Billy said. "Ain't you ever hid from someone?"

"He's always out walkin' at night," Heather said. "He's really weird."

"His parents never take him anywhere and he can't drive," Billy said. "I'd walk, too."

"He can't go to town because he raped some girl once," Gina said. "At the fair."

"Underneath the grandstand," Heather added.

"I doubt that," Billy said.

"He did," Gina said. "Ma said so. She said if Danny Boyer ever comes around, we should run like hell into the woods."

"He'd catch you," Billy said.

The girls stared.

Billy laughed. "You just don't know him," he said. "Danny's a nice guy." Billy slowed the tractor and pretended to turn the wheel. "In fact, why don't we go back and you can—"

Both girls screamed and grabbed onto Billy.

Laughing, Billy drove toward Riverbend.

At the river Heather walked straight to the big rocks, climbed up and began to take off her clothes. "Well, kids?" she said. The sunlight was behind her. Gina looked at Billy. "There's mosquitoes here," Gina said, and went out of sight around the rock.

Heather laughed at Gina. Then she said to Billy, "Maybe there are."

"Are what?" Billy said.

"Mosquitoes."

Billy smiled. "Nah," he said, "I don't see any."

Heather grinned, turned and dove. Rapidly Billy shed all his clothes and jumped in after her.

They swam there, Gina and Billy and Heather. Gina kept her T-shirt and panties on. The three of them paddled around each other in circles, spitting water, playing tag and water hide-and-seek among the rocks. Whoever was it had to count to twenty. Once, while Gina was counting, Heather swam up behind Billy and put her arms around his waist.

Billy tried to reach behind for her, but she laughed and splashed away.

Gina opened her eyes and called, "Ready or not!"

"Not," Heather called, paddling close up behind Billy again. "Count again," she said to Gina. "To fifty this time."

As the sun set they were suddenly cold. Shivering, they put on their clothes and climbed back aboard the tractor. It was late. Billy turned the tractor toward home. "Hey—I didn't get my cigarettes." Heather said.

Billy kept driving.

"You said you'd take me to Bob's."

Billy glanced once at the sun, which was already low and orange.

"Unless you're chicken," she taunted, and turned away.

Billy braked the tractor, made a full turn and headed back down the road toward Bob's Barn.

"Who-ee!" Gina called.

It took twenty minutes to reach the Barn. Billy pulled in and stopped by the far side of the parking lot, in the shadows. He noticed Dale Schwartz's El Camino parked there, along with a bunch of other local trucks and cars. "Hurry up," Billy said to Heather.

Another pickup pulled up. Locals. They nodded at Billy, took a longer look at Heather, in her wet T-shirt.

"Sure," Heather said. She fluffed up her hair as she walked slowly toward the lights of Bob's.

Gina ran alongside Heather. "I want a Mountain Dew."

"You don't have any money," Heather said.

"Neither do you," Gina said.

"So?" Heather shrugged.

Billy waited outside. A pickup pulled in and parked not far away; two men got out. Billy pretended to examine the tractor's steering wheel. The men tossed away cigarettes and went toward the tavern. Behind Billy the sun was gone now, the sky turning purple. Moths circled the humming yard light and fluttered on the ground beneath it.

He waited several more minutes, then walked up to Bob's. In the store part, Heather and Gina were nowhere to be found. The tavern part was a new addition without windows. At the back was a bar with red and yellow beer lights and a jukebox. Gina was playing pinball. A can of Mountain Dew sat on the glass, and two quarters lay beside it. At the table nearest the bar, Heather was smoking a cigarette and sipping a Coke. Minors could not sit at the bar, but they could sit close to it. And on a bar stool near Heather sat Dale Schwartz. He had some dollar bills and change spread out on the glass table.

Billy stared. Schwartz was not wearing his black mechanic's cap. In the dim light of the barn his black hair shone with oil of some kind, probably his own. He wore a white cowboy shirt with several buttons open. He had a skinny and darkly hairy chest. He laughed loudly and said something to Heather.

Billy jerked his head at Heather. "Come on," he whispered.

She ignored him.

He went over to Gina. She looked up briefly—then back down at her game.

"Get Heather," Billy said. "We gotta go."

"You get her," Gina said. She swore, then fed another quarter into the machine.

Billy walked over to the bar.

"Well if ain't the number one hay boy, Billy Baggs," Dale said. He looked bigger, taller sitting on the bar stool. His beady black eyes focused on Billy.

"Heather, we gotta go," Billy said.

"Hey, I didn't know you two were on a date," Dale said. A few people turned to look.

"It ain't no date," Heather said.

Her breath smelled sweet. Sweeter than just Coke. It was the same whiskey smell that Billy remembered on Dale Schwartz's breath.

"She don't want to go," Dale said to Billy. "So you better run along, Billy-boy."

Billy stared a moment at Heather. She turned away and blew smoke out of her nose. In the corner, Gina, her tongue clenched between her teeth, played the pinball machine. Billy stopped beside her.

"Talk to Heather."

"Why should I?" Gina said. She didn't look up.

In the purple twilight Billy started up the tractor and headed home. Alone. The little H had no lights, but he took it safely across the highway and then onto the county road. He drove at full speed. Down the slope past the river the night air was damp. It smelled like water and reeds and swamp. A raccoon scurried across the road in front of him. Billy swerved to miss it. Up the hill, toward high ground, the air warmed. Finally he came to the field gate and his own land. It was dark now. A moon was rising.

He drove—slowly—up the lane to the barn. He saw Abner come out onto the porch. He stood there. He was outlined by the kitchen light behind him. Billy parked the tractor in the shed and trotted toward the house.

"Where the hell you been?"

"Trappin'. Lookin' around."

Abner squinted. "Lookin' around, eh? Maybe I ought to look around a little myself—like at the gas tank."

The tractor was put away. Clear across the yard. "Go ahead," Billy said. He met his father's gaze.

Abner glared at him for a long moment. "Get on up to bed now," he said. "I'll get to the bottom of this in the mornin'."

CHAPTER TWENTY-TWO

Billy set his little windup alarm for midnight and tucked it under his pillow. It was a hard lump beneath his ear. He let his eyes drift shut and saw Heather. On the big rock, the sun shining in her red hair, the sun shining between her legs. He shifted in bed, had to lie on his back.

He made himself think of other things.

Like baseball. Tomorrow there was no hay to bale, which meant he might be able to go to town. Might. It all depended. . . .

The alarm clock rattled in his pillow like a snake under a log. Quickly Billy smothered it. Found the button. He blinked and squinted at its face. Midnight already.

He had been dreaming some baseball dream: the curving red dirt of the pitcher's mound, the shaggy green edge of the infield grass. He shook his head to clear it.

He listened, then slipped into his clothes. He eased down the stairs. He made sure to avoid the next-to-last step, which creaked. Outside, in the moonlit yard, Skinner stirred in his doghouse.

"Good boy," Billy whispered. "It's all right."

In the machine shed Billy found a gas can. Carefully he poured about two gallons into the tractor's tank.

Next there was the problem of the gopher traps. It was his good luck to have a bright moon outside. He got his bicycle and headed down the lane. Skinner shuffled along beside him, waking up as he trotted. In a few minutes they reached the wide, silvery hayfield. He found his sack of traps by the rocks.

In the pale field the gopher mounds were black eyes. Billy rode toward the nearest mound and got off his bike a few yards away. Skinner sniffed the air. One of the mounds was blacker and taller than the rest. It grew even as they watched. There was a steady scratching sound. Tiny sprays of dirt rose one after another. It was not an eye but more like a little volcano rising in the field.

"Easy, boy," Billy said to Skinner. As they walked closer, the scraping sound stopped. The gopher disappeared down its hole, but it left its tunnel open. A gopher would always come back to plug up its mound.

Billy fished out a trap from the sack. He wound its spring, set its trigger and slid it into the hole. The traps were the Death Clutch brand, round and narrow wire contraptions made especially for pocket gophers. Billy pulled out a small rod from his sack. He anchored the trap so the gopher wouldn't drag it underground. Then he looked across the field for the next village of gopher mounds.

In short order he and Skinner had set ten traps. Twice Skinner galloped ahead and tried to grab the gophers, who were way too fast for him.

"Cut it out; you're no damn owl," Billy said.

But soon enough he had emptied the bag of traps. They were all set. Billy went back to the rock pile to wait. Skinner lay beside him. Billy leaned against Skinner's warm side. His eyes slipped shut. As he dozed there, once or twice he thought he heard noises. Car noises.

Then voices . . .

He stared sleepily off toward the road, but saw nothing.

Baseball took over his dream. . . .

"No, don't! Stop it!" someone said.

Billy sat up suddenly. He had been rounding third base. He blinked his eyes. The moon had swung lower in the sky; at least an hour had passed. The field was empty and quiet, like it had been before. He listened but heard nothing.

"Come on, Skinner," he said, shaking his head to clear it. "We got to check our traps."

He went to the first set and pulled out his trap. A fat gopher, as big as a man's hand and still warm, drooped in the trap. Skinner whined.

"No way," Billy said. He dropped the gopher into his sack.

Traps two, three and four also had gophers in them. One was still alive and squirming. Billy stepped on its head until there was a cracking sound and it was dead.

Number five was plugged tightly with dirt, as were six and ten. The rest all had gophers.

"Seven for ten," he said to Skinner. "We're battin' seven hundred, boy!"

Skinner wagged his tail briefly. He looked off toward the road.

"Fifty cents times seven is three fifty."

Skinner kept staring toward the tree line and the road.

"What is it, boy?" Billy said.

Billy shaded his eyes from the bright moon. The road gate lay open. He was certain he had closed it. Farther off, by the trees, moonlight glinted off something. A car No, a pickup. Billy laid his bike on its side and came closer. He eased around the rock pile, stayed low among some small pines, then leaned out for a better look. It was a pickup. Dale Schwartz's El Camino. Inside he could hear a noise, a sniffling noise, like someone was laughing. Or crying.

"Shut up!" Dale said. "You know you wanted it."

The sniffling noise continued.

"You got hot pants, that's your problem, not mine."

There was a sharp, slapping sound.

"Why, you little bitch!"

There were thudding sounds.

A voice cried out sharply. A woman's, or a girl's

voice. It sounded like Heather!

Billy's heart leaped into his throat. He felt blood pounding in his ears.

"You tell anybody, there'll be real trouble," Dale said loudly. "You got that?"

Billy looked around. He had to be sure. He began to sneak along the brush row toward the truck until he was twenty yards away.

Suddenly Skinner yipped.

There was silence in the pickup.

Billy froze.

There was a clanking sound, and the door swung open. Moonlight glinted off a rifle barrel. Dale Schwartz peered out into the field.

Billy didn't breathe. With his free hand he slowly squeezed Skinner's mouth shut. He waited.

"Coyote probably," Dale said finally. He took a another look across the field. "Coyotes are easy pickin's for me. I can drill one right in the eye from two hundred yards. They never know what hit 'em," he said. He turned back to the pickup. "Makes you wonder what that feels like, don't it?"

There was silence, then another sniffling sound. Dale went around the truck. A door slammed.

Billy crept closer. He still couldn't see clearly.

"Anyway, we better get out of here. Old Man Baggs will think I'm stealing his dirt or somethin'." The engine whirred, and the pickup lurched forward. Billy jumped out of the brush, but the pickup was long gone. It sped away west, disappearing without head-lights into the shadow of the trees.

"Dammit," Billy said. He hadn't seen the girl, but he could swear it was Heather's voice he'd heard.

Heart thudding, Billy found his gopher sack. He pedaled home and made it safely into bed. But he just lay there with his eyes open.

CHAPTER TWENTY-THREE

"**R**ise and shine!" Abner's voice boomed up the stairs.

Billy groaned and squinted at his clock. It was five thirty. He thought of Heather and sat bolt upright.

It was a dream.

It wasn't a dream.

It was a dream.

"You better check them gopher traps you spent so much time last night settin'," Abner added.

There was silence at the bottom of the stairway.

Billy stared at the ceiling. He let one leg fall from the bed. With his foot he stamped the floor twice. "I'm up," he said.

When the front door slammed, and his father's footsteps receded, Billy hopped out of bed. He went to the little window that looked out on the yard. He watched Abner limp across to the machine shed, head toward the little tractor. He saw him screw off the gas cap, dip a stick into the tank, then pull it out and hold it up to the light. Billy watched a moment, then turned away.

Downstairs, he grabbed a quick bowl of Cheerios. Mavis was up and around as usual. Luckily she didn't ask him any questions. She was too busy getting ready for work.

Soon he was headed down the lane on his bike. The sack of gophers and traps was heavy over his shoulder. Just out of sight, he hung the sack in a tree, then sped across the field on his bike. He went to the far corner of the farm, to the field gate.

There, in the grass, were the tracks. Four spots where the grass was still flat. Four tires stopped for a long time. Billy squinted closer at the ground. Something small shone in the dirt. Billy leaned down and picked up a rifle shell. An empty brass casing, .243 caliber. He looked down the road, then put the shell carefully in his pocket. In the bushes something else glinted. An empty bottle of Jim Beam. Billy squatted down beside it. Sniffed it. He scrunched up his nose.

It took him fifteen minutes' hard riding to get to the Erickson house. The sun was still low and orange, and reflected off the windows of the faded white trailer house. A rooster crowed but that was the only noise.

Billy parked his bike in the ditch and sneaked along the side of the trailer house. The back windows, the bedrooms, were quiet. Through a smaller window he heard water running. And sloshing noises. Then it was quiet. He inched closer, looked inside. Nobody.

At the front of the trailer a door clicked open. Billy peeked around the end of the trailer. It was Heather. She looked around, then headed to the clothesline. She began to hang up some clothes. She held up a pair of white panties. She looked at them, then pinned them to the line. Billy stepped out.

"Christ!" Heather called. Then she covered her mouth and looked toward the trailer.

"Sorry," Billy said. "I didn't mean to scare you."

"What the hell are you doin' sneaking around here at six thirty in the mornin'?" she snapped.

Billy stepped closer. "Last night—" he began.

"What about last night?"

"Well . . . I was out after midnight. Gopher trappin'. It's a long story. But in the west forty, by the trees . . ."

Heather swallowed. "What are you talkin' about?"

"I saw Dale Schwartz's El Camino."

Heather bit her lower lip. "Who?"

"Dale Schwartz."

Heather looked away, down the road, then back. "So? He's always out parkin' with some woman."

"I heard your voice. You were cryin'."

Heather stared at Billy. Then she laughed shrilly. "Me? My voice? In Dale Schwartz's truck?"

Billy nodded.

"You're nuts, Billy, really nuts," Heather said.

"It was you," Billy said. "I know it was you."

Heather's mouth opened. For one long moment Billy thought she was going to tell him something.

"Get the hell out of here—you don't know any-thing about nothin'!" Heather shouted. She ran at Billy with her fists up. Her eyes shone wet in the sunlight.

Billy took several hits on his arms. She was crying now, hitting him harder and harder. Billy broke away and ran across to the ditch. He leaped on his bike and pedaled away. Heather stopped chasing him at the edge of the garden. Looking back, Billy saw her stand-ing there, arms limp at her side.

And behind her, framed in the screen door of the trailer, was another, smaller figure. Gina.

By the time Billy returned on his bike, Abner was midway through milking. "So let's see them gophers," Abner said, standing up beside a white cow, milker in hand.

Billy reached into his sack. He laid the first one on the concrete floor. "One." Then "Two . . . three."

Abner stared.

"Four, five . . ."

Billy laid out all seven in a neat row.

"Seven," Abner said, swinging the shiny milker to the next cow. "Out of how many traps?"

"Ten."

"What happened with the other three?" his father said.

Billy shrugged. As he put the gophers back in his sack, he suddenly asked, "How old is Dale Schwartz?"

Abner looked up. "Twenty-five or so."

Billy nodded.

"Why do you ask?"

"Just wondered."

Billy waited with Mavis for Mrs. Pederson. They stood by the mailbox and looked down the road. Mavis glanced at her watch. Billy carried his old baseball mitt and a brown bag with his lunch. Mavis was dressed up again, in a dress he hadn't seen before.

"I wish she'd come," Mavis said. "I don't want to be late."

"She'll come," Billy said.

"When I get that Chevy. . . ." Mavis murmured.

As they waited, the meadowlark called again. Then it was silent. Billy was just about to tell her about Heather and Dale Schwartz—about what probably had happened—when Mrs. Pederson's car came into sight.

"There she is," Mavis said.

Mrs. Pederson's brown Ford coasted toward them, then rolled several yards past, its engine silent. As they walked forward, Mavis said cheerfully, "Billy's along again today, if you don't mind."

Mrs. Pederson squinted her small eyes at Billy. After a pause she said, "I suppose there's room."

"Hurry up, then," Mavis said to Billy.

He took the backseat.

"I do try to keep the weight down," Mrs. Pederson said as they very slowly accelerated down the road. "The lighter your car, the less gas it takes, wouldn't you agree?"

"It makes sense to me," Mavis said. She winked at Billy.

Billy did not wink back. He was looking off down the road. Thinking.

"I have good tires and I never carry a spare," Mrs. Pederson said. "I figure if I ever have a flat, one of my neighbors will come along and help me."

"That's what neighbors are for," Mavis agreed. She glanced again at Billy.

"One thing with living in the country," Mrs. Pederson said, "is that you can always trust your neighbors."

"Absolutely. Wouldn't you agree, Billy?" Mavis said. She was trying to make him smile.

Billy only gazed out his window. He didn't even hear what she said.

CHAPTER TWENTY-FOUR

Dale Schwartz lay on his creeper underneath a '58 Ford with a leaking transmission. He squinted past his trouble light. Maybe the transmission case was cracked. More likely a seal had given way. In the background his radio played, but otherwise the shop was silent. He liked it that way. Especially when he had a hangover like this one.

He worked. But slowly, like some faraway change in the weather, he got the idea he was not alone. Suddenly he looked to the side.

"Jesus!"

His head jerked up and struck the muffler. Stars whirled and burned in his eyes. Beyond the stars, at ground level, was a face.

A round, white face with red hair.

Gina Erickson.

Hot Pants Heather's little sister. He had gotten Heather to put the brat Gina to bed last night, then slip out and meet him down the road. A pint of Jim

Beam and a few cans of Coke was all it took. But this, this could only mean trouble.

"I know what you did," Gina said.

"Say what?" Dale said. Because of his hangover, and from looking sideways through the trouble light, he thought this might be a bad dream.

"To Heather."

"What are you talkin' about?" Dale asked. "I gave you kids a ride home."

Gina said, "More than that. I know what you did."

"Did what? Are you crazy?"

"I know," Gina said.

Dale tried to sit up, and hit his head again. Stars flared brighter this time. He lay back and blinked them away. "You're nuts. I dropped the both of you off and then went home."

"Huh-uh," Gina said. She shook her head. "Heather snuck out later. I saw her go from my window. And you took her out somewhere, got her drunk. And more. I know what you did."

"Dammit," Dale said, recovering himself. He tried a grin on her. "You're the one's been drinkin' too much. Too much of that Mountain Dew. I should never a bought you all that pop last night. It gave you bad dreams, kid."

"Huh-uh," Gina said. "It weren't no dream."

"You got any proof?" Dale said, sharply this time. He would have to try another track with this girl.

"Heather was throwin' up all night. And cryin'. And washin' out her clothes this morning."

"So? That don't mean nothin' to me," Dale said. He found his wrench and pointed it at Gina. "You go around accusin' people of things, you better have more evidence than that."

"I got evidence," Gina said.

"Beat it before I get mad," Dale said, turning back to work. "I got a transmission to fix."

"You're too old to be out with Heather. You could go to jail for a long time," Gina said.

"I'm gonna count to ten," Dale said.

"Twenty years, minimum, for what you did. I saw it on TV."

"One," Dale said.

"With no parole."

"Two."

"On TV there was a witness."

"Three."

"I got one, too."

Dale Schwartz looked over at Gina. "Sure," he said. "You just told me you stayed home."

"It weren't me. It was somebody else saw your truck parked in Old Man Baggs's field."

Dale swallowed.

"He came up close and he heard you and Heather. He saw everything. He knows."

With a jerk, Dale pulled himself out from under the car. He staggered upright and went around the Ford after this brat. But there was no one there. Outside he heard a bicycle rattle. He saw her flying down the road, then across the field.

CHAPTER TWENTY-FIVE

oach Ozzie Anderson, arriving early at the ball field, saw a body in the dugout. Someone was curled up on the wooden bench. At first Ozzie thought it was the town drunk. Or perhaps a high schooler after his first keg party. Or, more likely, a former Flint athlete trying to relive better days.

That last type Ozzie had found there before, high school stars who had left Flint and gone on. Gone on to college athletics where, for various reasons, they had not made the grade. Gone on to jobs in Fargo and the Cities, Minneapolis and Saint Paul, where they did not like living. And so they came back to Flint on weekends. Sometimes they called Ozzie from a bar, their voices slurred. And sooner or later they ended up at the ball field.

The field where life had been simple.

The field where a man knew which base to run to.

The field where a man always knew if he was safe or out.

At night among the mosquitoes, and with tiny

bonfires, the faded stars of yesteryear relived the old games.

The good catches.

The long hits.

The bad calls. Lots of bad calls by umpires and referees.

And they drank beer and vodka and smoked grass until they tipped over, out for good this time, on the long wooden bench.

But this morning, the body in the dugout had bright-yellow hair on a head pillowed by an old, fat-fingered baseball mitt. It was Billy Baggs.

Coach Anderson clumped down the steps and dropped his duffel bag.

No movement from Billy.

He began to rack bats, rattling them in their slots.

Suddenly Billy sat up and blinked. He saw the coach and jumped to his feet.

"Oh, there you are, Billy," the coach said. He turned as if he hadn't seen Billy.

"I was just . . ."

"Checking your eyelids for holes?" the coach said with a smile.

Billy rubbed his face.

"Tell me—how much sleep do you get on the average?" the coach asked, turning to the bat rack.

Billy blinked. "Um . . ."

"Well, try to get more," the coach said. "We wrap up the season this Saturday. A big game with Buckman. Doug Nixon is gone on vacation with his parents. We need you."

Billy said, "We got thirty acres of hay down. The last of it, and . . ."

The coach waited.

"We'll be balin' tomorrow. All day. And if we don't get it done, we'll have to finish on Saturday." Billy frowned and looked out at the sky, which was clear and cloudless.

The coach thought a moment. There was no practice tomorrow. Sheila was in Wisconsin. He had planned on going fishing. "You'll get that hay put up," he said. "I just got this feeling."

Toward the middle of practice Billy looked up from third base. A yellow-and-white El Camino approached the field. Dale Schwartz. Billy froze.

The ball bounded past Billy and rolled toward the fence.

"Hey, Baggs, wake up!" Coach Anderson called.

Billy trotted after the ball. He watched the El Camino from the corner of his eye. The shiny pickup passed slowly by on the street. Hardly moving. Like the driver was looking for something. Or someone. But the El Camino kept moving, passing on toward the Feedmill. Billy squinted after it as he returned to the infield.

There they were beginning a new drill, quick-release throws for the double play. The coach demonstrated. He took a throw with his glove hand. He kept his throwing hand close beside the glove. The ball seemed to ricochet from the glove pocket into his bare hand. Then he fired the ball back to first base.

"Okay, let's try it," Coach Anderson called. "Remember, quick release but no errors. Fundamental ball says get the first out."

The coach trotted back to the plate, then chopped a grounder to short. Dusty Streeter scooped and threw. At second base Shawn Howenstein caught the ball and fired to first. A quick release but a low throw, which Jake Robertson dug out of the dirt. "Okay, double play!" the coach called.

Billy looked back to the street. Dale Schwartz's El Camino was parked by the third-base fence. Fifty feet away. Right behind Billy.

Inside, Billy saw Dale's short silhouette. Saw the rifle hanging in the rear window.

"Okay, third to second to first," the coach called. "Baggs to Howenstein to Robertson." He laced a grounder to Billy.

Billy bobbled the grounder, then threw without control. The ball spun from him toward the foul line and the fence.

"Everybody's safe," the coach called.

Billy trotted to pick up the ball. Dale Schwartz stared at Billy. Billy met his gaze for a moment, then picked up the ball and turned back to the field.

"Once again," the coach called.

Billy looked over his shoulder once more, then set himself. The next grounder he scooped and threw—two feet over Shawn's glove at second.

"Head in the game, Baggs," the coach called.

Billy looked over his shoulder at the pickup. The coach looked, too.

"Okay, let's take a break," the coach called.

As the boys went to the water cooler, the coach walked over to the El Camino. "Morning," he said. He had thought it was somebody Billy knew. Or maybe even a scout from Buckman. But he recognized the short, dark man as a local. He knew him from somewhere. Ozzie never forgot a face.

"Morning, Coach. How are your boys doing this year?"

"So-so. We're six and five on the season. One game left."

The man nodded. He squinted across the field to the boys. "I thought I'd stop for a few minutes. One of my neighbors plays for you."

"Oh, yeah? Who's that?"

"Kid by the name of Baggs."

"Billy." The coach nodded. "He's new."

"How's he look?" the man said.

"A little rough," Ozzie said, "but the potential is there."

The man in the El Camino said, "I seen him miss a couple there. Kid's kind of a night owl. He probably don't wake up till midafternoon."

"Funny you should say that," Ozzie said, glancing across at Billy. "I found him asleep in the dugout this morning."

The little dark man squinted at the coach. Then he looked across at Billy. A slow grin spread on his face. Ozzie tried to recall where he had seen this man.

"Tell Billy-boy that Dale came by," the man said.

He suddenly started his car. "Tell him I take a special interest in my neighbors."

"All right," the coach said. "Dale Schwartz," he added.

"Pretty good memory," Dale said. He grinned briefly.

The coach stared. Dale Schwartz. Class of about 1960. The coach had been a young teacher then, but he remembered the face. He could see Schwartz in the back row of his social studies class, a sly, bad apple–type student, a thief of some kind, if his memory was correct. And something about a sixth grade girl, when Schwartz was a junior. Some kind of trouble. Schwartz had not finished school. Ozzie glanced over to Billy, who looked quickly away.

"Anything else?" the coach asked.

"Nope," Dale said.

"Thanks for stopping by," the coach said. He watched the El Camino purr away.

CHAPTER TWENTY-SIX

The next morning Billy lay underneath the baler. At nine o'clock the sun was already hot on his legs. As he worked the grease gun, hay chaff fell in his eyes. He rubbed them and spit. Suddenly Skinner began to bark. They heard car tires crunching on the gravel. Abner muttered, "Now who would that be?"

Billy slid out from underneath the baler. He looked down the driveway. A small blue car came into the yard. A Toyota. Billy had seen it somewhere. A town car. He squinted. The driver was a large man wearing a Twins cap. "The coach!" Billy said.

Abner frowned.

The coach drove right up. "Morning, gentlemen," he called out his window.

"What does he want?" Abner muttered. He looked at Billy.

"I dunno," Billy said. "I swear."

The coach shut off his engine, got out and trotted over. Before he could speak, Abner said, "Billy can't play any baseball today. We got hay to bale."

"You're right, he can't play baseball. There's no practice today," the coach said. "That's why I'm here."

Abner looked sideways at Billy.

"Billy said you'd be baling today. If you can tolerate a city slicker, I thought I'd give you a hand."

Abner glanced at Billy, then down the road. "I've got hay help comin'." He looked at Ozzie Anderson. "And besides, I can't afford city wages like you're used to."

"I'll do it for the exercise," the coach said.

Abner stared at the man. "You'd bale hay for the exercise?"

The coach winked at Billy. "Sure. Just for the fun of it. Plus one small thing."

"I knew it," Abner muttered.

"Tomorrow there's a ball game. The last of the season. I'll work today if Billy can play ball tomorrow."

Abner thought about that. He checked the sun, then looked down the empty road again. He spit and tipped back his hat. "You know what I'd like? One a them new balers. The kind that makes those big, round bales. The baler drops them in the field, then you come by later and pick them up with a tractor and loader. From start to finish, one man is all you need."

"But today it looks like you need a hand, and here I am," the coach said. He produced a pair of leather gloves from his hip pocket.

Abner squinted at the gloves. "You might end up in the hayloft. I can't have no stranger fallin' off the wagon and gettin' run over."

"I've worked in haylofts," the coach said.

"It's gonna be ninety-five in the shade," Abner said. "Way over a hundred in the loft."

The coach looked at the barn. Heat waves shimmered off its wide front. "So I'll sweat off a few pounds," he replied.

"You could stand to," Abner said, glancing at the coach's belly.

Billy looked at the ground. Coach Anderson chuckled.

"I'll warn you," Abner said to the coach. "We work all day. We don't stop but for food and fuel."

The coach put on his gloves. "I'm your man."

"All right," Abner said with a grin. "We'll see about that."

At nine thirty, Abner drove over to get Big Danny Boyer. Dale Schwartz had not shown up, and did not answer his phone.

"So what's the story with Dale Schwartz?" the coach said.

"Nothin'," Billy said immediately.

"He came to the field yesterday."

"A neighbor guy." Billy tied off the new bale of twine, trimmed the ends.

"He seemed mighty interested in you."

Billy was silent.

The coach let it drop. He looked around. "Nice place you got here."

Billy shrugged.

The coach spotted the granary, and Billy's target

on the side. There was the painted outline of a batter, and the boards were broken at his belt line. "That what I think it is?"

Billy nodded, and held back a grin.

"Looks like you need a catcher. You got any brothers or sisters?"

Billy's smile faded. "No," he said abruptly. He turned away and began to roll a hay wagon toward the rear tongue of the baler.

The coach trotted over to lend a hand. Afterward he said, "Show me around the place."

He followed Billy around the sawmill.

The corral.

The outbuildings.

And the main building, the barn. Inside it was neat but dim and low-ceilinged. There was no pipeline milker. No electric barn cleaner. The tall silo had no unloader. Everything on this farm was done by shovel and fork. Coach Anderson looked at Billy's hard, brown arms.

Outside, tires crunched on gravel as Abner's pickup returned up the driveway. Big Danny sat in back. His yellow head stuck up over the cab.

"Schwartz's place is locked up. Nobody around," Abner said. "He's probably run off with somebody's wife again. Either that or he's too drunk to get home. So I guess it's just us, boys."

The coach stepped up to Danny Boyer, who wore his usual ragged clothes and busted-out shoes. "Good morning, I don't believe we've met. I'm Ozzie Anderson." He put out his hand.

Danny Boyer shrank away from the coach like a dog from a club.

Thanks to Dale Schwartz, Big Danny would not go into the hayloft, so that chore fell to Coach Anderson. As the coach climbed the ladder, Billy said one last time to Abner, "Let me take the loft. Put the coach on the wagon."

"Nope," Abner said, staring at the coach with a gleam in his eye. "The hayloft is the place for him. He can't get hurt there. Plus it'll teach him about real work for a change." Abner started up the tractor and headed toward the field. Billy kicked dirt, then leaped aboard.

The baling went smoothly. In the dry heat Billy loaded the wagon, then drove it to the barn and the empty one back to the field. When the coach came down from the loft for noon dinner, he was pink-faced and wet with sweat. Little rivers ran off his face and down his neck. His shirt was soaked through.

"How's it goin' up there in the loft?" Abner asked, as he dished out hot potatoes.

"Fine," the coach said. He took one small potato.

"You better eat," Abner said.

"Watching my weight," the coach said. He winked at Billy and passed him the bowl. His eyes had reddened from dust.

Billy noticed the coach's hand. Across his palms the hay-bale twine had raised blisters like white mushrooms. The coach made conversation, but Billy kept watching the little bites he took, the way he flinched when his fork handle touched the mushroomed skin.

At three o'clock, when Billy brought in another full wagon, the coach did not come to the doorway for air. The thermometer on the pumphouse read an even hundred degrees in the shade. As he switched wagons, Billy kept watching. No coach. Billy hopped down from the tractor and went up the ladder. In the loft hay chaff hung in a thick, dusty green fog. The coach lay back on the bale, breathing heavily. A square, perfect wall of hay rose behind him.

"Coach?"

"Hey, Billy," the coach said, sitting up. His face was crimson. Almost purple.

"Come on down for a spell. Get some air."

"I'm all right," he said. "Really." He nodded to the towering wall of bales. "What do you think? Do I pass the hayloft test?"

"It weren't no test."

"Wasn't any test," the coach said.

"Right," Billy said.

"Anyway, I'm a stubborn Norwegian," Ozzie said. "Keep 'em coming."

"Okay," Billy said uncertainly.

At six o'clock Billy came in with wagonload number twelve. The hayfield was empty but for wagon tracks. And the thermometer read 102 degrees.

Billy scrambled up to the loft to help the coach finish. The heat there hit him like a wall of steam. In the gloom, Ozzie Anderson sat on a bale, staring. He was

235

panting rapidly—like Skinner when he had run five miles—in fast, shallow breaths. There were blotches of even darker color on his cheeks. His eyes ran black at their corners with alfalfa dust.

"You all right?" Billy said, peering into the gloom and dust.

The coach nodded. "Sure, Billy," he whispered. He kept up that fast panting.

Below, from his tractor seat, Abner called out, "How are things lookin' up there, coach?"

"Fine," the coach croaked. "Just fine."

"Jesus, you better quit, coach! Go on down," Billy said.

Big Danny started up the conveyor, and the chain began to rattle again.

The coach shook his head.

"I'll get this last load," Billy said. "Go get some air."

"No way," the coach said. He got up. He swayed on his feet like a punch-drunk boxer. He steadied himself against the conveyor and squinted down at the rising bales. "You got to finish what you start. Especially when you're almost there." He coughed, spit green and grabbed for the first bale. "Almost there," he whispered.

In twenty minutes the conveyor chain came around empty, then clattered to silence. The only sound in the loft was the coach's steady wheezing. Billy walked ahead of him to the door. He was afraid the coach might fall out and break his neck.

On trembling legs the coach came down the ladder.

In daylight his face was redder than a stoplight. His clothes, top to bottom, were black with dust and sweat.

Abner waited at the bottom. The two men looked at each other. "Twelve hundred and eighty bales," Abner said.

The coach nodded.

Billy was not certain the coach could speak.

"That's a pretty good day," Abner said, grinning at the coach.

"It's a record!" Billy said. "It's the most we ever put up."

"Still daylight left," the coach whispered, gesturing toward the fields. He managed a lopsided smile.

"Hell, I shoulda cut more hay," Abner said, pulling off his gloves. "Especially If I'da known *you* were comin'."

The coach looked down at his own gloves, then decided against taking them off. There were dark patches in the palms: blood.

Abner saw them and raised an eyebrow.

"Gloves nowadays," the coach said hoarsely. "They aren't what they used to be." He turned and headed to the long cattle-watering tank. There he stripped off his shirt and splashed great handfuls of water over his face, his neck, his barrel chest. Then he dipped himself half in the tank, and came out shaking off water like a big seal.

He returned to the barn, cleaner and breathing not quite so hard now. "Well, I'd better get back to town," he said to Abner. "Unless you got one last load."

"Nope. That's it." Abner's eyes flickered to the coach's hands. Abner cleared his throat. "I appreciate the help," he said.

"No problem; got to go," the coach said, sounding more like himself now. He headed to his car, managing a limping trot. There he reached in through the window for something. "Oh, Billy," he called.

Billy went over to him.

"This is for you. For tomorrow."

Billy looked inside the sack. Through its paper sides the sun shone on a red T-shirt with black letters that read FLINT SPARKS # 30, along with gray pants and black stirrups.

When Billy looked up again, the coach was driving away. Shirtless, his hair slicked back, he held on to the steering wheel with only his fingertips.

Billy held the uniform up to his face. It smelled fresh and new.

CHAPTER TWENTY-SEVEN

As the coach drove away, Abner said, "For a city slicker he put in a good day's work."

Billy closed his bag and started to turn away.

"What's that he gave you?" Abner said.

Billy shrugged. "Some stuff for the game tomorrow."

"Let's see."

Billy opened the bag and pulled his red jersey out halfway.

"What else?" Abner said.

Billy took out the gray pinstriped pants and the black stirrups.

"Is all that paid for?"

"Yes," Billy said.

"How?" Abner squinted at Billy.

"I worked out for it, in town," Billy said.

Abner nodded. He looked at the stirrups. "You know how to wear all that stuff? Those fancy leggings?"

"I can figure it out," Billy said.

"Well don't ask me if you can't," Abner said. "I never had a baseball uniform."

They headed in for supper—Danny, too—but the house was quiet. The oven was cold. Mavis was not yet home.

Abner looked at his watch. "Where in the Sam Hill . . . it's nearly seven o'clock!"

At that very moment a horn tooted and tires came fast on gravel up the driveway. They went to the screen door.

"Now who in the hell would that be?" Abner muttered. An old, shiny blue Chevrolet Impala braked to a halt.

Billy cleared his throat.

Mavis got out.

"What in tarnation?" Abner said.

"Hi, everybody," Mavis called out, reaching for two sacks of groceries, then heading up the porch steps.

Abner seemed frozen in place.

"How'd it go today?" Mavis said pleasantly.

Abner pointed behind her. "Whose car is that?"

Mavis smiled brightly. "Mine," she said.

Abner's eye widened. His jaw dropped an inch.

"Hi, Danny," Mavis said. Danny grinned goofily and opened the screen door for Mavis.

Mavis rolled right past them. "Don't stand in the way—I got frozen food here."

They gave way.

Abner stared at the car.

"Sorry I'm late," Mavis said. "I had to go to the courthouse and get the registration taken care of, license plates and all that."

Abner's jaw pumped once or twice but no words came out. Mavis began to bustle about the kitchen, turned on the oven. "But I bought some of those TV dinners," she said, rattling the sacks. "I thought we'd try them out. They say TV dinners are just the thing for a working mother."

Abner, still staring at the Chevy, murmured, "We don't even have a TV."

CHAPTER TWENTY-EIGHT

Chores ran late that night. First there was supper, the four of them, including Danny Boyer, sitting at the table eating from the TV dinners. Roast beef, peas, potatoes and a small red slice of candied apple. Abner kept glancing at Billy.

Then at Danny.

Danny finished his tray in about thirty seconds; afterward, he looked around the kitchen for more.

Billy, too, was nearly done, and it seemed like he'd just started.

"These TV dinners, they're not all that big," Mavis said.

Abner stroked his chin.

Billy bit his lip to keep from smiling.

"Well, they are supper," Abner said, "so I ain't complainin' none, but—"

Billy held his breath.

"But these are the worst damn excuses for food I ever ate, that's what!" Mavis said. She stood up. "Give me those." She went around and scooped up the trays whether they were finished or not and threw them in the trash. "Danny, go to the garden and get me a big onion. Billy, get me a dozen eggs from the cellar. Abner, get that block of cheddar cheese and grate up a pound."

They all snapped into action.

And fifteen minutes later they sat down to a real supper, one of Mavis's omelettes. It was thick, yellow and steaming, like a pie but twice as big.

"Tasty," Abner said, smacking his lips at the first bite.

"Really tasty," Billy added.

"Don't rub it in," Mavis said. She smiled behind her fork.

"What do you say, Danny?" Abner said. "Omelette or TV dinner?"

Danny speared a steaming wedge of omelette and stuffed it into his mouth.

They did not start milking until eight P.M. The cows milled around by the back barn door, hooting for their grain. It was nearly nine thirty, with the sun just touching the west tree line, when they finished up. "You go on in," Abner said to Billy. "I'll rinse the milker."

Billy trudged, head down, toward the house. Twelve hundred bales of hay, now the chores. He was beat. Whipped. Done in.

"*Psst!*"

He looked up, toward the sawmill.

"*Pssst!*"

Skinner woofed from the porch steps. Billy went toward the lumber piles. Gina stepped out.

"What you doin' here?" Billy said.

"Heather," Gina said.

"Where is she? What about her?" Billy said quickly, looking behind Gina.

"She ain't here. But she wants you to meet her. Tonight."

"When?"

"Midnight."

"Midnight!" Billy groaned. "Where?"

"At Riverbend. The path."

"Look—I can't," Billy said. "I got a game tomorrow and I got to—"

"You better come," Gina said. "That's what Heather told me to tell you. You'd better."

Billy stared.

His alarm rattled under his pillow at eleven thirty. Billy dragged himself from bed and slipped on his clothes. In a few minutes he was bicycling down the road in faint moonlight. Skinner loped along beside him. "This better be worth it," Billy said.

He woke up soon enough in the cooling, humid night. Mosquitoes and other night bugs brushed his face. He squinted his eyes against them as he rode.

Soon he was in the shadow of the woods, where it was very dark. On the trail to Riverbend he walked his bike. In the occasional patches of moonlight, he saw car tracks in the dirt. Recent car tracks. He squinted ahead through the gloom. Next to him something heavy *whoosh-whoosh*ed down from a tree, then glided silently through the trees.

"Owl," Billy said to Skinner.

"Psst!"

Billy stopped. Gina, then Heather, came from behind the trees and stood in a clearing.

"What's goin' on?" Billy said.

The girls were silent.

Skinner whined, sniffed at the trees nearby.

"You know what's goin' on. The other night. You and Heather," Gina said.

"What about me and Heather?"

"You know."

"What!" Billy said, exasperated. "Swimmin' you mean? We've done that lots of times." Heather would not look up at him.

"Not that," Gina said.

"So what, then?" Billy said. Skinner whined again. "Shut up!" Billy said.

"Later, after we went to Bob's Barn, what you did to Heather."

Billy stared. Then he laughed once before he turned to Heather. "You better tell your sister what really happened. Who it really was."

"I did tell her," Heather said.

Her voice sounded funny, like she wasn't herself now.

"She said it was you," Gina said.

Billy stared. "You two are crazy, really crazy."

"I wouldn't say that."

Billy whirled around.

Dale Schwartz stepped out from the shadows. "No, I wouldn't say they're crazy at all," he said.

Skinner growled.

"Watch your dog," Schwartz said, "or he'll get a slug in his brainpan."

"What are you doin' here?" Billy asked.

"Presidin' over a little meetin'," Dale replied. His teeth glinted in the moonlight. "A little meetin' of the neighborhood kids so as we get some facts straight."

Billy was silent.

"About the other night," Dale said, stepping toward Billy. "You and Heather. You young kids, you just got carried away, I guess."

Billy stared.

"Right, girls?"

Billy saw Heather's throat move as she swallowed.

"Right, girls?" Dale said, louder.

"Yes," they whispered.

Dale turned to Billy and shrugged. "So there you have it," he said. "I guess that leaves me out of this whole deal. Not that there was a big deal to begin with . . ."

Billy stared.

"So if you want to get Billy-boy here in a heap of trouble—and Heather, too—just feel free to spill the beans. On the other hand, if you don't want any trouble of any kind, I'd let things ride."

The clearing was silent.

"It's up to you kids entirely."

Billy, Gina and Heather were silent.

"Right?" Dale said.

The girls nodded. Gina sniffed back tears.

"Right, Billy?" Dale said.

"You ain't gonna get away with this," Billy said.

"With what?" Dale said. "Nobody seems to know just what it is we're talkin' about. Just what is *this*?"

Billy bit his lip.

They were all silent.

"Well that's that, then," Dale said. "If there's no further business . . ." He stepped back into the shadows and reappeared with a rifle. Billy jumped back.

"Sorry! Didn't mean to frighten nobody. It's just that I like to drive around at night when the moon is high and I can't sleep, and look for varmints," Dale said. "Lot of varmints out at night. But then you know that already, don't you, Billy-boy?"

Dale swung his rifle and fired into the trees. Yellow fire spit from the barrel, and the report snapped in the clearing. Heather and Gina flinched, then huddled together. "Damn," Dale said, staring into the darkness. "Thought I saw a varmint."

Billy swallowed. He stepped closer to the girls.

"That's good," Dale said. "That's touching, really. You three ought to stick together. Otherwise you might end up in all kinds of trouble. If you know what I mean." With that he turned and walked down the trail out of sight.

"Quick," Gina said. Billy and Heather followed her into the brush. They crouched there. Mosquitoes whined and bit at their ankles and necks and faces. Then Billy heard the El Camino start up and purr softly away.

"We'll get him," Billy said, standing up.

"No!" Heather said quickly.

"He can't get away with this!"

"He already has!" Heather cried. "Don't you see? He already has!"

That night, back home, Billy could not sleep. He lay there, eyes open, until the rooster crowed.

CHAPTER TWENTY-NINE

Billy helped his father with morning milking. Kneeling in the straw alongside the last cow, he waited for her to finish and leaned his head against the Holstein's big flank. It was solid and smooth and warm. . . .

The next thing he knew, Abner was roughly shaking him. ". . . fall asleep, you'll get kicked in the head," his father was saying. "Then I won't have any help on this goddamn place."

Billy rubbed his eyes and quickly wiped drool from the side of his mouth. He stood up and removed the vacuum hose, then shucked loose the teat cups. Air squawked, then sighed away. Stepping forward to pour milk, Billy stumbled, and a splash of steaming milk spilled over the side. The barn cats, ever alert, leaped forward to lap up the overflow.

"What the hell's the matter with you!" Abner said. "Give me that milker. You better wake up more than that if you figure on playin' ball today."

Billy gave way to his father, then kept his distance the rest of milking. Abner seemed in a rage today. A rage larger than spilled milk or an extra trip to town could cause.

At breakfast Billy's father was completely silent. He ate staring down at his plate. Mavis didn't say much, either. Billy didn't get it; he thought things were going all right this summer. Abner had all the hay in. Mavis had her job and her car. But today there was some dark cloud hanging over everything; it was like he had done something bad he didn't know about.

At nine o'clock, Billy slipped upstairs to get dressed. He took his time putting on his baseball uniform. With each part of it—the T-shirt, the pants, the stirrups—he forgot more and more about the gloominess in the house. He checked himself in the round mirror on the wall. The mirror was small and he could never see his whole self, but part by part he watched himself change into a baseball player. A real baseball player.

Just as he was finished dressing, he heard Mavis's footsteps on the stairs. She tapped, then appeared in the doorway to his room.

Billy shyly stood facing her in his uniform.

His mother stared at him. "Oh Billy, you look nice!"

And then began to cry.

Billy stared. And then in one instant the air went out of him. He looked at his calendar and it was all clear to him. Today was Robert's birthday.

"I'm sorry, Billy," Mavis said quickly. "I didn't mean to—"

Billy's face went hard and tight. He turned away. He sat down on his bed, looked out the window. He could see the field.

Mavis watched him. "Don't," she said, taking him by the shoulders, turning him. Turning him around hard. "Don't do that." But then she cried again into her hands.

Slowly Billy stood up. He began to take off his uniform. He didn't care if his mother saw him in his underwear, he didn't even think about that. He just wanted the uniform off.

Mavis looked up. "No, Billy!" she said. She grabbed him by the shoulders so hard his head rattled. "You're playing ball today. You need this, don't you see? The timing is just bad luck—that's all. You're going to play and you're going to do fine and we're all going to do fine."

Billy let Mavis hold him for a while. He stood there, arms limp, his mother holding him, rocking him.

"I'm so sorry," Mavis said.

Over her shoulder, through the window, he could see the field.

And then it was time to go. In the yard, Abner was nowhere to be seen.

"We have to say good-bye," Mavis said.

They found Abner by the sawmill. He was splitting wood. Blow after blow with the heavy splitting maul.

"Billy and I are heading to town, now," Mavis said. "Billy has his game today."

There was silence except for Abner's splitting. The wood cracked and popped and splinters flew. Blow after blow.

"Look at him!" Mavis said suddenly to Abner. "At least you've got to look at your son!"

Abner slowly put down the maul. He turned toward them. He was sweating, his face shiny, his shirt blackened at the armpits. He took off his cap and stared at them. At Billy. But it was like he didn't see them at all.

On the highway they listened to the radio in Mavis's Chevy. "Go ahead," Mavis said, "pick a station. Any station you like." She smiled hopefully at Billy.

He slowly rolled the dial. A Beatles song came on.

"What do you think of the Beatles?" Mavis said.

Billy listened. "They're okay."

"I think they're great," Mavis said.

They drove for a while. She kept glancing over at Billy. Finally she said, "He'll be all right. It's just that this day is always hard for him. Tomorrow he'll be fine."

Billy was silent.

CHAPTER THIRTY

As they passed Randy Meyers's A-1 Cars, and then the Flint city-limits sign, Billy began to tug at the legs of his uniform. Test his stirrups. Check himself once, then twice, in the side mirror of the Chevy. Not butterflies but whole birds started to flap about in his stomach. Suddenly, there was the school and the baseball field.

Mavis motored into the lot just as King Kenwood arrived in his family's Cadillac convertible. The two drivers parked next to each other. Mavis stared at the Cadillac. "It must be nice," she remarked to Billy.

Her window was open, and the Kenwoods turned to stare.

"Excuse me?" King's father said. He wore a yellow leisure shirt with a wide collar.

"I said nice car you've got there," Mavis answered cheerfully.

"Thank you," Mr. Kenwood said, smiling now.

"Kind of reminds me of something Elvis would drive."

Mark Kenwood's eyes widened. Billy made haste to get out.

"Have a good game, Son," Mavis said, snagging Billy at the last moment and planting a loud kiss on his cheek.

"Geez, Ma!" Billy complained, and escaped to the field.

On the field the Buckman Warriors, dressed in blue, were already warming up. The weather was sunny, warm and dry, and cicadas buzzed in the park among the tall elms. It would be very hot later in the afternoon, but this morning was perfect for baseball.

Billy, self-conscious in his uniform, walked up to Tiny Tim, Butch Redbird and the others.

"Hey, King. Hi, Billy."

From the dugout Coach Anderson turned to look.

"Baggs—you're lookin' sharp today," Butch said.

"You look like Jim Kaat," Jake the Fake said.

"It's true," Dave Nelson added.

"Uncanny!" Tiny Tim chimed in.

The other players all agreed.

"Could I get somebody to warm me up?" King Kenwood muttered. "Anybody?"

Butch trotted over to King, and Coach Anderson gave Billy a smile and a quick thumbs-up sign. A small grin spread across Billy's face.

"Okay, let's warm up, boys," the coach called, getting up stiffly from the dugout bench.

"Hey—what happened to your hands, Coach?" Tiny Tim asked.

The players looked. Coach Anderson's hands were puffy white and crisscrossed with Band-Aids.

"My wife caught me smoking." The coach winked at Billy.

"Come on, really," Tiny Tim said.

"Two lines, boys; let's go," Coach Anderson said.

As Billy did toe-touches, he kept looking at his black stirrups. At the gray pinstriped pants. They were wool, but somehow were not hot or itchy. The sun shone down on his back. On his neck. Maybe he couldn't feel anything. Maybe he was paralyzed. Maybe this was a dream. Off to the side he saw the umpire arrive—a real umpire with a little black beanie and heavy chest pad.

Beside him, Tiny Tim said, "Hey, Billy—did you know you're starting at third?"

Billy turned to look at Tim.

"Really," Tim said. "I saw the lineup. Plus you're batting third."

During throwing and infield warm-ups, the bleachers steadily filled. There were even some cheerleaders, including Suzy Langen with her long blond ponytail. Mavis sat dead center. Around her was a crowd of mothers and fathers. More fathers than mothers.

Coach Anderson blew his whistle, and the Flint Sparks hustled to the dugout.

"Here's the deal, boys. Win today, and we're

headed to the play-offs. Lose, and we're done for the season."

There was brief silence.

"Let's get 'em! Come on!" The team suddenly exploded. On the field the umpire was dusting off the plate with his little brush in quick strokes.

"Doug Nixon is gone on vacation with his parents," Coach Anderson continued, "so I've moved people around some. Billy Baggs is at third."

Billy swallowed as the coach continued with the rest of the lineup.

"Any questions?"

The boys were silent.

"So it's simple, boys," the coach said. "Go out there, remember your fundamentals, play hard—and one more thing."

"What's that?" Tiny Tim said.

The coach looked around, then lowered his voice. "The cheerleaders are here, so let's make sure your flies are zipped."

The boys laughed loud and clear (but checked themselves), then burst onto the field. There was a great cheer. Billy looked up at his mother again. He thought of Abner at home, swinging the splitting maul.

Blow after blow.

Suzy Langen led several other town girls in a cheer:

> *"King, King, he's our man.*
> *If he can't do it, Butch can!*

Butch, Butch, he's our man.
If he can't do it, Jake can!"

"Play ball!" the umpire called. He tossed a clean white ball to King Kenwood. Billy watched the baseball float toward the mound; it gleamed white in the late summer air, and the game was on.

But King Kenwood was not.

He walked the first three batters. "Bear down, Archer!" shouted his father from the stands. "Bear down, son!"

"King, King, he's our man . . ." the cheerleaders called weakly.

The fourth batter cracked a sharp double to the center-field wall that cleared the bases. Three runs in. Man on second.

The crowd groaned.

King turned his back and rubbed up the ball for a long time, then got the next batter on a ground out to first. For some reason, the runner held at second.

The following batter rapped a chopper to Billy. Because of yesterday's twelve hundred hay bales his legs felt heavy and his hands thick—but he managed to knock down the ball. The Buckman base runner had gambled on a base hit, and was running. Billy tagged him barehanded, then fired a high smoker to first that Jake Robertson hauled down just before it went orbital. Rough, yes; ragged, yes—but a double play.

There was cheering in the bleachers—loud cheering from one person in particular. Billy heard Mavis's strong voice above the others. And King Kenwood trotted off the mound, though not before nodding Billy's way.

The cheerleaders conferred briefly. They seemed confused.

Mavis called down loudly to them, "Billy's the name—Billy Baggs." Then she put two fingers to her lips and whistled. The cheerleaders giggled, and went into their routine:

"Billy, Billy, he's our man . . ."

The Flint lineup read this way:

SS	Dusty Streeter
2B	Shawn Howenstein
3B	Billy Baggs
C	Butch Redbird
LF	Curt Hadrava
RF	Ricky Jokela
CF	Dave Nelson
1B	Jake Robertson
P	Archer Kenwood

Tiny Tim Loren lead the cheering for Dusty Streeter, who led off. Lance Brewster, the Buckman pitcher, was a square-shouldered, thick-chested kid who scowled down at Dusty. His first pitch was high and inside, and put Dusty on his back.

The Flint dugout crowd hooted and jeered at the

Buckman pitcher. Dusty got up and slowly brushed himself off.

"Dusty, Dusty, he's our man . . ."

Dusty pointed his bat at the Buckman pitcher and said something. The umpire trotted out and spoke to both boys.

On the next pitch, jeers turned to cheers. Dusty hacked the ball past Brewster and into center field: base hit.

"Shawn, Shawn, he's our man . . ."

Shawn Howenstein came to the plate ready to hit. He took the first pitch on a long ride to left field—but not long enough by a step. The Buckman left fielder hauled down the ball on the run at the fence.

And Billy came to bat.

"Billy, Billy, he's our man . . ."

He swung at the first pitch, which was in the dirt.

"Swing at strikes, Billy," the coach called from the dugout.

Billy set himself and took the next pitch. Called strike. Now 0 and 2. He glanced behind him, at the stands. Mavis held one hand to her mouth. Billy set his jaw and dug in.

He fouled the third pitch hard down the third base line. The contact felt good and he had seen the ball well. He readied himself for the next pitch.

"Watch out for junk!" King Kenwood shouted.

Billy, looking for a fastball, loosened his grip

slightly at Kenwood's warning and held back his weight. The Buckman pitcher, with a lot of fake motion, threw a floater.

Billy watched it come. The ball drifted toward him, as fat and slow as a snow goose settling into decoys. Billy waited, then pistoned forward off his rear leg. He swung, head down, following the ball all the way onto his bat—and crushed it. The ball disappeared so fast he lost sight of it before it left the infield. He raced toward first, where Tiny Tim, the base coach, was hopping up and down, pointing at center field and making chirping noises. Billy rounded first and kept running. He still couldn't see the ball.

So he just kept running hard.

The Buckman center fielder waited at the fence, and Billy kept running. He streaked toward third. He heard shouting but kept running. He rounded third and blazed into home with a long slide and a great cloud of dust.

The Sparks greeted him with great whooping.

"Good hit, Billy—though we're gonna have to work on that home-run trot," Coach Anderson said.

Everybody laughed.

Billy turned around and looked at his teammates. A home run! He looked down at his new pants—he had ripped out one knee.

"Don't worry, we'll get it sewn!" the coach said.

His teammates crowded around and escorted Billy back to the dugout. They laughed and slapped him on the batting helmet so much that he did not get a chance to look up at his mother. But he could certainly hear her!

After things had quieted down, Billy glanced at King Kenwood.

"Thanks," he said.

King, staring out at the field, was silent.

After the first inning the pitchers settled down. Innings two and three saw the score go to 4–3, then 5–4, Buckman's favor. Billy got another base hit, but in the fourth inning there was trouble.

Big trouble.

King Kenwood took a hard liner in the right kneecap. He went down shouting. His father raced onto the field, arriving even before Coach Anderson. They worked on King, who was soon up and around with a purple bruise. He limped to the dugout.

The Sparks groaned.

Jake the Fake hurriedly warmed up.

And there was more trouble still. Billy, with some time to look around, spotted Dale Schwartz on the top bleacher. He was watching Billy through binoculars. Quickly Billy looked away. His heart began to pound, but he made himself stay calm. He was in the dugout. There were the white lines of the playing field. Inside it the green grass. Nobody, not even Dale Schwartz, could bother him during a baseball game.

Jake the Fake took the mound. He was replaced at first by Dave Nelson. Jake walked in two runs without coming close to the strike zone. Buckman, 7–4.

Coach Anderson let Jake walk two more Warriors before trotting to the mound for the ball. "Sorry," Jake said.

The coach smiled. "Next time," he said to Jake, and took the ball.

Jake trotted off, replaced by Curt Hadrava, a right-hander; this sent Tiny Tim Loren to left field.

Curt Hadrava could throw strikes no better than Jake the Fake. And soon it was 10–4 in the top of the fourth.

After the Sparks had finally gotten out the side, their dugout was silent. "Strikes, gentlemen, my country for some strikes!" Coach Anderson muttered. The players looked down at the floor as Tiny Tim Loren dragged a bat toward the plate.

"Dig in," the coach called, recovering his attitude. "Make contact. Let's go, now."

Tiny Tim swung wildly, and with his eyes closed— and miraculously blooped a single into left field. He stood in the batter's box, staring.

"Run! Run!" the Sparks screamed.

Tiny Tim blinked, then scampered to first base just in time.

"My nerves," Coach muttered. "I should have been a mailman."

With the help of three Warrior errors, the Sparks picked up three runs in the bottom of the fourth, but in the top of the fifth the Buckman Warriors scored five more times, for a 15–7 bulge.

"Or maybe a train engineer," Coach Anderson murmured to himself. "Or a librarian."

While on the bench during the long fifth inning, Billy noticed a maroon Highway Patrol car drive up to the field. "There's your dad," the other Sparks said to Dave Nelson. Dave tried to act cool. Harold Nelson gave his son a two-fingered salute as he went up to the stands. Billy thought about that, how nifty it would be to have a father who carried a gun. In the bleachers Dale Schwartz, his eyes on the highway patrolman, eased out the other side. Billy saw him slip away through the crowd and head for the parking lot.

Next time up, in the bottom of the sixth, Billy whacked a solid double to right center. But that was the only action, and the Sparks went into the seventh inning with Curt Hadrava on the mound. After Curt walked the first batter, Coach Anderson trotted to the mound with Butch Redbird, then motioned for Billy Baggs to join them.

"Want to try a batter or two?" the coach asked Billy.

"Me?" Billy asked. "Pitch?"

"He might as well," Curt said disgustedly.

"It's okay, Curt," Ozzie said, smiling. "Next time, all right?"

Curt nodded and kicked at the dirt.

"So what do you say, Billy?" the coach said.

"I don't know," Billy said to the coach. "This is my first game. . . ." He looked up at the stands.

"What the hell, go for it," Butch Redbird said.

"What the *heck*," Coach Anderson said automatically.

Billy smiled a little.

"Just throw to Butch like you did to me that morning at the field before anybody came," the coach said.

Billy rubbed his neck and swallowed. "Okay, I'll try it."

"So what's your specialty?" Butch said. "Curve, knuckler, spitter?"

The coach winked at Billy, then jogged off to make other substitutions.

"Naw," Billy said to Butch. "I just throw it."

So in the top of the seventh, with nothing on the line for the Flint Sparks except the last three outs of their summer, Billy Baggs took the mound. The crowd had thinned. A good many people had left for the beach, for the lakes. Those who remained in the bleachers were nearly all parents. Mark Kenwood turned to another father and said, "This Baggs boy, who is he? Some farm kid?"

A strong voice answered. "That's right. And I'm Mavis Baggs, his mother."

The fathers looked up at Mavis, then at each other, then back at the field.

On the mound Billy took some warm-up throws. The first two sailed over Butch's head. The third bounced in the dirt. Butch hustled out to the mound.

"Do you hunt?" Butch said.

Billy said, "Uh . . . yeah. Sure."

"What kind of gun you got?"

"A twenty-two single-shot," Billy said.

"Gopher killer," Butch said with a nod.

Billy smiled.

"See this glove?" Butch said.

Billy stared at it.

"It's brown. It's fat." He made it open and shut, wiggling its body. "It's alive!"

Billy grinned. He turned away and began to rub up the ball. Then he retook the rubber and fired a strike. And two more to finish his warm-ups. The ball cracked with a whipping sound against Butch's glove.

The Buckman coach turned to look over his shoulder at Billy. His dugout slowly went quiet. The leadoff batter looked back uncertainly at his coach.

"Batter up!" the umpire called.

Billy stared down at Butch, then drilled the first pitch right in the pocket. The batter was a yard behind in his swing.

The Flint Sparks jeered.

"Smoke him, Billy!"

"Burn him!"

Which Billy did.

The batter, standing back as far as possible from Billy's fastballs, managed one foul ball, then struck out.

Coach Anderson leaned back in the dugout and smiled. Billy Baggs's first strikeout. He found his clipboard and jotted down the batter's name—Josh Johnson—the date and even the time of Billy's first strikeout.

Billy stood on the mound and smiled. He looked around proudly.

Which brought the Buckman bench alive.

"Hotshot on the mound!"

"Bucktooth hotshot!"

Billy's smiled died. For an instant Coach Anderson thought Billy was going to leave the mound and duke it out with the whole Buckman team.

"Get the batter, Billy!" the coach called. "The batter. Focus on the batter."

Billy looked down at the ball in his hand, then retook the mound.

The second batter went down on three pitches. He did not appear to see any of them. The slap of Billy's third fastball echoed off the brick face of the school. The Buckman dugout and the spectators, too, went quiet.

"Time!" Butch Redbird called. He trotted to the dugout. There he found a leftover sweatsock, which he wadded up inside his glove. "Baggs is gonna put me on the disabled list," Butch said. "I'll never play the piano again."

"Or hold a cigarette," Jake added.

The coach smiled.

During this short break, Dave Nelson's father, the highway patrolman, left the stands and went to his car. He turned on his radar gun and focused its invisible beam on Billy Baggs.

Another vehicle arrived. A pickup. An old dusty pickup with a man inside. A man wearing a greasy cap low across his forehead.

For the last batter, Billy pitched from a full windup, the kind he used back on the farm, when he was alone, in the evening. Alone except for Robert, who always watched him from somewhere. Billy could feel Robert right now. He could feel Robert's presence. He could feel him watching.

Billy's right leg kicked shoulder high as he slung himself forward.

Butch rocked backward, and dust puffed from his glove.

"Stee-rike one!" the umpire called.

The batter stepped farther to the safe side of the box. He looked at his coach.

"Stand in there!" the Buckman coach shouted angrily. "Stand in there!"

The batter swallowed and dug in at the outside of the batter's box.

Billy kicked higher still, whipped down his arm and blazed another fastball.

Butch grunted at the blow in his glove.

"Stee-rike two!"

The batter crouched protectively, ready to dive for cover.

Billy put everything he had into the last pitch. He kicked high—almost as high as Sandy Koufax—and then followed with the whiplash of his arm. The ball was a white-hot comet. Dust exploded in Butch's glove and he went backward to one hand—but held it.

"Stee-rike three—he's out of there!"

Billy looked around, then followed his team off the field. Mavis, her voice even louder than before in the near-empty stands, cheered and whistled. Billy did not permit himself to look up into the stands.

In the dugout, as casually as he could manage,

Coach Anderson said, "Nice job, Baggs."

Billy nodded.

"And by the way," the coach asked, "is that a scout in the stands? That guy by your mother?"

Puzzled, for a crazy moment thinking of Robert, Billy stepped out to look. He froze.

There was his father.

Abner was there.

He was sitting right beside Billy's mother. He had come straight from the woodpile, and among the other fathers he looked like an old hobo—but Billy didn't mind and Mavis didn't either. Billy could only stare at his father.

Who nodded. One nod and a small, proud smile for Billy.

EPILOGUE

And so, that last game of the season, the Flint team had final at bats. They managed two runs, but the score ended with Buckman 15, Flint 9. The baseball summer was over.

The teams lined up to exchange handshakes, and the coaches brought up the rear. Buckman's coach, Rick Allen, a younger fellow with a mustache, pulled Ozzie aside. "Who *was* that last kid?"

"My secret weapon," Ozzie said.

"Seriously, where did he come from?"

"I brought him up from my farm team," Ozzie said, his eyes shining.

Afterward, Coach Anderson gathered the boys for his postgame conference, gave them his Next Year speech and finally set them free. But the boys were in no hurry to leave, and neither was he.

Ozzie leaned in the doorway of the dugout. A few parents came by. Ozzie shook hands with them, wincing because of yesterday's blisters. Abner Baggs had already headed to his pickup, which was not surprising. But at least he had come.

The Sparks clustered again around Billy. Billy was grinning his crooked-tooth grin. He was happier than the coach had ever seen him. Butch re-created the weakling swings of the last Buckman batters, and the boys laughed; Billy, too. All of them were there except King, who had gone to get an X ray he probably didn't need; they were laughing, leaning in on each other, bumping against each other.

And for a moment, Ozzie Anderson saw the future.

This was the team.

This was the one.

Billy Baggs and King Kenwood alternating on the mound. Butch Redbird behind the plate. Dusty, Shawn, Doug and Jake in the infield. Outfielders he had plenty of. When they were all seniors at Flint High, that was the team that would—but Ozzie stopped himself. With boys it was a mistake to assume anything. He could not assume they would all be at Flint High four years from now.

He could not assume that they would all be playing baseball four years from now.

He could not assume they would still be alive four years from now; he had been a coach and teacher long enough to know better. In Flint, with its farm machinery and snowmobile and hunting accidents, it was more than likely, four years from now, that at least one of these boys would be dead.

But at this moment they were all very much alive. The sun was high and shining and their voices echoed from the dugout and across the field. Gradually they collected their gear, still talking and laughing. Ozzie watched them disperse.

Butch Redbird to his crazy-looking bike and no parents that Ozzie had ever seen.

King Kenwood gone in his Cadillac with his father the lawyer and his mother the dental technician.

Tiny Tim Loren to his grandmother and his psychiatrist.

Shawn Howenstein to the butcher's shop, to its carcasses and cleavers.

Dusty Streeter to his mother, who spent her nights in the bars and did not seem to mind that her husband was in Vietnam.

Billy Baggs to his rough-and-tumble farm, to his fork and shovel.

As Ozzie gathered gear, Harold Nelson came out to the field. "Nice season, Coach," he said.

"Thanks."

Nelson pointed to his patrol car. "In the last inning, just out of curiosity I put the radar gun on the Baggs kid. I thought I'd try to see how fast he was throwing."

Ozzie nodded.

"What do you think he clocked?" Nelson said.

Ozzie thought a moment. He looked back at his boys heading off on their bikes. Laughing, calling to each other on this blue afternoon of late summer. He was suddenly struck by how young they were: They were barely teenagers. "I'm not sure I want to know," he said softly.

Nelson paused, then looked off at the boys for a long moment. "I can understand that," he said, nodding. He turned back to Ozzie. "I'll make it my secret, then. You wouldn't believe his speed anyway, and I guess neither do I. I'm going to take that gun in and have it tested."

"You do that," Ozzie said, smiling.

They shook hands, and the patrolman turned away.

When everyone was gone, Coach Anderson swept out the dugout. Its pine bench had sharp new carvings on it. This year's names. In a few years these carvings would be worn smooth, too. Layers upon layers of names. Boys come and gone. He ran his hand down the bumpy script of the plank, for good luck. He felt the names, he saw their faces. At the far end of the bench he smiled down at the newest name: Billy Baggs.

Finally he took a last look around, then picked up his bags. The dugout was to be left open, of course.

Someone might need it.

Trudging across the field, he looked up at the sky. A single yellow elm leaf came floating down. He stopped to watch it drift. It lit just on the edge of the outfield grass. Summer was over, yes. But there was next summer. There was always next summer.